Ki held his breath, listening again for the noise. It was the faint squeak of soft footsteps against the long wooden porch outside the window.

"I heard it," Jessie whispered.

Having left his *tanto* and his vest with throwing stars by the door, Ki knew he'd have to rely on the lethal arts of the *ninja*. He darted out of the study and toward the entry hall, hoping to beat the stalker to the unlocked door.

He was too late!

The doorknob began to turn slowly. The door swiveled open on its quiet hinges. Ki prepared to strike like a cougar. He gestured for Jessie to step back into the common room. She retreated, but not soon enough.

"Jessica Starbuck," said a deep voice. "I've found you."

WESLEY ELLIS

LONE STAR
AND THE SCORPION

JOVE BOOKS, NEW YORK

LONE STAR AND THE SCORPION

A Jove Book / published by arrangement with
the author

PRINTING HISTORY
Jove edition / March 1995

ISBN: 0-515-11570-3

A JOVE BOOK®
Jove Books are published by The Berkley Publishing Group,
200 Madison Avenue, New York, New York 10016.
JOVE and the "J" design are trademarks
belonging to Jove Publications, Inc.

PRINTED IN THE UNITED STATES OF AMERICA

10 9 8 7 6 5 4 3 2 1

★

Chapter 1

A golden sun was slipping behind the western horizon when Jessica Starbuck stepped on the porch of her comfortable ranch house. She knew she should be tired after a day of rounding up stray calves for branding, but somehow she was strangely invigorated by the work beneath a broad West Texas sky. Maybe it was the satisfaction of working her own land, the Circle Star ranch, which stretched as far as the eye could see in all directions; or maybe it was the weather, which teetered awkwardly between the final gasps of winter and the first breath of spring. She pulled off her leather riding gloves and slapped them against the denim britches that fit snugly around the curves of her rounded hips and the length of her shapely legs. Each snap of leather against denim produced a wisp of dust and a reminder of how good a hot bath would feel tonight.

With her free hand, she loosened the leather thong that snugged her brown, flat-brimmed hat over the tresses of her copper-blond mane. She pushed the brim until the hat slid down the back of her slender neck to her shoulders, where the leather thong caught it. As she shook her head, the sun's dying light played off the copper tones, which streaked through her hair and accentuated the pure green of her eyes.

1

Beneath her denim jacket and workshirt, her full bosom rose with each breath and fell as gently as the soft breeze that came from the west. Her full lips parted into a smile as she thought of the spring transformation of the Circle Star ranch. Already, the green of new grass was emerging from the soil, and ribbons of spring flowers streaked the land like a shattered rainbow fallen to earth.

Of all the business endeavors that fell under the purview the Starbuck empire, not one brought her more pleasure than the Circle Star. She sighed at the memory of her father, Alexander Starbuck, the man who had built Starbuck empire from a single San Francisco curio shop into a major import-export business operating between the United States and the Orient. What Alexander Starbuck had started in a ramshackle building on the San Francisco waterfront eventually had become a massive empire with interests that stretched from coast to coast and with influence that reached across both the Pacific and the Atlantic. But for all that he possessed and all that he could purchase, her father had loved best this West Texas spread. On the Circle Star he had built his home. On the Circle Star he had raised his daughter. And on the Circle Star, Jessie had developed into a woman with her mother's beauty and her father's business acumen.

As her thoughts lingered on her deceased parents, Jessie failed to hear the soft pad of rope-soled slippers as Ki approached. The sound of his voice startled, then embarrassed her.

"You think of your father and mother," Ki said as he stepped up onto the porch.

Jessie stood surprised, not so much from his silent approach as from his theft of her very thoughts. "How did you know?"

Ki nodded serenely, but withheld his answer for a moment, patience being a virtue among the samurai. His dark, almond-shaped eyes stared not at Jessie but through her. His shoulder-length black hair framed a Eurasian face that hinted of his Japanese mother and his American father. His raven eyebrows and the pencil-thin mustache that followed the curve of his mouth accentuated the tawny hue of his face, even in the dwindling light of day.

"How did you know, Ki?" Jessie repeated.

"A disciplined mind will observe more than the eye can see," Ki answered.

If anything, Ki was certainly disciplined, Jessie thought. Trained in the martial arts, he possessed the discipline of a samurai warrior, not to mention the cunning of the *ninja*. That discipline and that cunning he had dedicated to the protection of Jessie after her father was assassinated by evil agents of a worldwide business and political cartel. Together Jessie and Ki had slowly dismantled the cartel until it was no longer the sinister threat that it had once been. If they had not destroyed the cartel, then they had at least shattered it into so many pieces that it was but an impotent shadow of its former power and wicked influence.

"The eye is an open window into the soul," Ki continued, "and a disciplined mind can see in that window. There was in your eyes the same look I have seen many times before when you talk of your parents. Just as untrained eyes can recognize a smile or a frown, a disciplined mind can recognize your thoughts."

Jessie smiled, believing but not fully understanding the way of the Oriental mind and the personal philosophy that sprouted from it. She had been around Ki too long to challenge his philosophy. And she knew that her life had been enriched by the philosophies of the Far East. The housekeeper who raised Jessie after her mother's death had in her youth been a highly honored Japanese courtesan. With the full blessing of Alexander Starbuck, the housekeeper had taught Jessie the sacred secrets of a whole woman's sexuality, secrets that were meant for sharing and enjoying with men.

There were times like these, after an invigorating day's work, when Jessie needed a man as much as she needed a meal or a bath. Her lips curved into a playful smile at Ki as she wondered what he must be like as a lover. Her

3

wonder was fleeting for that would never be, could never be, as they had developed a familial relationship. Since the deaths of their parents they had been the only family each other had. She was as dedicated to him as a sister and he was as protective of her as a brother. When she had saddled up to help the Circle Star's hands with the ranch chores today, Ki had accompanied her even though he disliked work from horseback.

"It was a good day to ride the ranch and work the land," Jessie offered, a tease in her words.

"Nature works the land," Ki corrected. "We merely ride it. As many business responsibilities as you have with the many Starbuck interests, I don't understand your desire to spend time working the cattle."

Jessie nodded as she watched the last sliver of sun disappear behind the horizon. "Even a disciplined mind must need relief on occasion. Riding the land makes me think better."

"Perhaps for you," Ki replied, stroking his chin, "but for me, it just makes me hungry."

Jessie laughed as she watched the golden glow on the horizon slowly fade. She enjoyed this time of day, when light gave way to the coolness of night. "Supper can wait just a moment more."

"As the business of Starbuck enterprises waited today," Ki answered with a friendly challenge in his voice. He stretched his arms and angled for the door to the ranch house. The windows of the ranch house were beginning to glow from the lamps the housekeeper lit as she moved from room to room.

Jessie turned and followed Ki inside, softly closing the door behind her. The aroma of roast beef and boiled potatoes from the dining room greeted her. She pulled her hat from around her neck and hung it on the rack by the door, then removed her jean jacket and tossed it on the seat of a nearby chair.

Ki pulled off his black leather vest with its myriad of pockets stuffed with the many *shuriken,* or throwing stars,

4

that he carried everywhere he went. He draped the vest over the back of the same chair where Jessie had left her jacket, then pulled from the waistband of his jeans the lacquered sheath that held his *tanto*, a small curve-bladed knife he carried everywhere. After dropping the knife atop Jessie's jean jacket, he straightened the black sash around the waist of his loose-fitting cotton blouse.

"We'll eat, then I'll attend to business," Jessie said as she entered the dining room and took her customary chair in front of a setting of fine china and silver.

Ki slid into the chair opposite her, and they began to help themselves to the fine meal the cook had prepared. The platters and bowls were generously filled, but both Jessie and Ki ate lightly as was their habit. They finished off the meal with baked cinnamon apples for dessert.

Folding her napkin and placing it on the table, Jessie rose and motioned to Ki. "Care to join me in the study and see that I take care of business?" Jessie thought she detected a hint of a smile that passed over his lips as he silently rose. Outside, the wind kicked up, and a sudden gust rattled the windowpanes. Maybe this was the approaching breath of another norther, she thought. She hoped not, preferring to have seen the last of winter's seasonal fury.

As she and Ki entered the great common room with its polished floors and its massive gray slate fireplace, Jessie glanced at the portrait of her mother, a beautiful woman with copper-tinged hair, a green dress to match her emerald eyes, and a smile that could melt stone. Each time Jessie passed the portrait, she felt a pride in her bosom that she resembled her mother. From the dining room now, Jessie could hear the sounds of her housekeeper clearing the dishes. Soon the housekeeper would draw water for Jessie's bath and put out additional quilts in her room in case the murmuring wind outside was blowing in another cold spell.

Jessie led Ki into the study, her favorite room in the house because it had been her father's office. The faint cherry scent of his aromatic pipe tobacco still reminded her of him. She had changed very little about the study, and still used his rolltop desk as her desk. At the battered desk, she read the correspondence and issued the orders that ran not only the Circle Star ranch but also various Starbuck ventures throughout the country. The desk was arranged with neat stacks of letters and papers, the day's mail having been placed by the housekeeper in the center of other papers.

"Not too much mail," she said as she slid into the swivel chair and began to thumb through the letters.

Ki eased into one of the soft leather chairs apportioned around the room and watched Jessie divide the letters into stacks.

"Nothing out of the ordinary here," she said to herself before she examined the last letter. Then she changed her mind. "Maybe I was mistaken." She held up the last letter for Ki to see.

Even from a distance, Ki could tell by its thick envelope embossed with a standing lion that the letter was important. As Jessie twisted the letter around, Ki saw that it had been sealed with wax.

Taking a letter opener from one of the desk's pigeonholes, Jessie slit the top of the envelope and removed a single page of stationery. Jessie frowned as she read the letter to herself, then looked at Ki before she read the missive aloud.

" 'Miss Starbuck, I will be staying in Galveston for several days and would like to invite you for a visit to discuss business of mutual interest. I regret I cannot visit you or be more specific, but my time is short and this business is too sensitive for correspondence. I shall look forward to your response and the ultimate pleasure of your company. Your humble servant . . . ' " Jessie paused.

"Who's it from?" Ki asked impatiently.

Jessie smiled. "I thought a disciplined mind could read my thoughts."

"Your thoughts, yes, but not your mail." Ki sat forward on the edge of his chair.

"It's signed by Lord Clinton Bly of Manchester, England," Jessie answered, a puzzled look upon her face.

Ki brought his hands together, his palms and fingers flat against each other. "The name I cannot place at the moment."

"Lord Clinton Bly is one of the world's great industrialists."

"Now I remember," Ki said. "Textiles, isn't it?"

Jessica nodded. "He got his start by taking over Manchester's textile mills, some say by less than honorable means. He expanded into shipbuilding, coal, steel, railroads, and more, again some say by questionable methods. Because of his business power, today he commands the respect of governments throughout the world."

"A rival then of the Starbuck empire?" Ki wondered aloud as he pyramided his fingers against each other.

"Not directly. Our spheres of influence are different." Jessie held the letter up to the yellow glow of the desk lamp and studied it. She wondered if a disciplined mind could read Bly's motives somewhere between the lines of his missive. What could he possibly want? Jessie possessed her father's shrewd business judgment, and was thus naturally suspicious of someone who approached her under the premise of "business of mutual interest." In her experience, the word "mutual" was often a cover to disguise motives that were better described as selfish.

She lowered the letter from the lamp, then refolded it and slipped it back inside its fancy envelope, which she dropped on the desk.

"Have you looked in the . . ." Ki began.

"I was about to," Jessie answered as she reached across the desk and pushed a wooden panel that slid away to reveal a secret drawer. She pulled open the drawer and brought out a black logbook, its leather cover slick from use and its pages well thumbed.

" . . . logbook?" Ki finished.

She turned page by page through the list of names her father had written in the book. Each name had a connection with the cartel. Most were crossed out after fatal encounters with Jessie and Ki. A few names still remained, but they were mostly of cartel foot soldiers who were insignificant in the absence of the leadership Jessie and Ki had decimated over the years in their crusade to halt the evil combine that had killed Alexander Starbuck.

Even though many of the names were aliases or cartel code names, not one seemed to have any possible connection with Clinton Bly, the industrialist. Jessie closed the logbook, slipped it back in its hiding place, closed the secret drawer, and then slid the panel back in place.

Ki pushed his palms together again and calmly awaited Jessie's answer.

"Nothing there to suggest Clinton Bly is involved with the cartel," she said.

"What then will be your answer to his lordship?"

Jessie stood up and walked slowly around the room, considering her decision. Bly was indeed one of the world's most powerful men. Yet, she was one of its most powerful women. She could go, but why should she? After all, the Starbuck empire had offices in Galveston. From those offices on The Strand, the street that was Galveston's financial district, Starbuck Cotton Exporters marketed and exported about two-thirds of all the cotton grown in Texas.

Perhaps Bly's inquiry related to her cotton exporting business. It was logical that Bly might want to meet her there, since Galveston was the headquarters for that operation. And if Lord Bly was interested in discussing cotton dealings, he could well deal with Martin Bark, the manager of her cotton operations.

Had it been another time of year, Jessie might have been more amenable to traveling to Galveston. However, she liked the ranch this time of year, relished its rebirth and enjoyed working the cattle before the weather turned hot and dry.

Turning to Ki, Jessie shook her head. "I plan to decline his invitation. He should speak first to Martin Bark in Galveston if he has business with me. Marty can be trusted to forward a message in confidence."

"Then tomorrow we can ride to town and telegraph your reply," Ki offered.

Jessie smiled. "You want to go to town so you don't have to spend another day riding the ranch."

"Now you are beginning to read my thoughts." Ki rose, the loose-fitting blouse parting at the top to reveal his muscled chest.

"Well," Jessie said with a shrug, "if we are going to have to make a trip to town tomorrow, perhaps I should go through the other mail and take care of any other business that requires it." Jessie retreated back to the rolltop desk and slid into the swivel chair to begin reading the rest of her correspondence. Upstairs she heard her housekeeper beginning to draw her bath. "You can go on, Ki, if you like," she offered.

Ki said nothing, and Jessie turned around to check on him. He stood motionless, as if he were in a trance, his attention focused on something elsewhere.

"Ki, you can go."

He looked slowly from the window toward Jessie.

Now Jessie wished she could read his mind, know what he was thinking. "There's no point in you staying while I finish up my business."

Slowly, Ki nodded as if he were distracted by something. "Perhaps I shall go. Good night."

Jessie turned back to her desk and picked up another letter to open, but before she could slit it open, she heard the soft patter of Ki's rope-soled shoes on the hardwood floor.

As she twisted around to see the problem, Ki was upon her, his hand sliding gently over her mouth as he blew out the lamp on her desk. The room went dark.

"Someone is out there," he whispered. "Someone is stalking us."

★

Chapter 2

Ki held his breath, listening again for the noise that had caught his attention. It was the faint squeak of soft footsteps against the long wooden porch outside the window. There it was again! He had been right. Someone was trying to sneak into the house. It wasn't one of the cowhands, for they knew better than to approach the house in the dark without first identifying themselves. Ki lifted his hand from Jessie's mouth.

"I heard it," she whispered.

Ki allowed himself a slow deep breath. Having left his *tanto* and his vest with throwing stars by the door, Ki knew he had to rely on *ninjutsu*, the lethal art of the *ninja*. Above all, he had to protect Jessie from this approaching danger.

He crept away from Jessie toward the rectangle of light entering the study from the great common room. With several lamps lit in the big room, Ki feared he had inadequate time to kill them all. He darted out of the study and through the common room toward the entry hall, hoping to beat the stalker to the unlocked door.

He was too late!

The doorknob began to turn slowly. Ki slid against the hallway wall and approached the door from the blind side.

10

The door swiveled slowly open on its quiet hinges. He took slow, deep breaths that prepared him to strike like a cougar.

Then he stole a quick glance toward the hallway, and caught a glimpse of Jessie holding her twin-barrel .38-caliber derringer. He shook his head for her not to use it. If this stalker had allies, Ki did not want them to be alarmed by a gunshot, not at least until Ki had found out everything he could from this intruder. As the door opened perpendicular to the wall, Ki gestured for Jessie to step back into the common room.

Jessie retreated, but not soon enough.

"Jessica Starbuck," said a deep voice, "I've found you."

Instantly, Ki jumped around the door.

"Huh?" came the same deep voice.

As Ki pounced upon his prey, he saw a man in a black hat and a black duster that hid his features, but not the lunge of his hand for a weapon. Ki grabbed his arm, then jerked the startled man toward him. With a quick foot in his path and a quicker flick of the wrist, Ki flipped the stranger in the air. The intruder landed flat on his back, his hat flying away.

Ki dove for the downed intruder, but he quickly rolled away. Ki bounced off the bare floor where the intruder had been as the stranger managed to get to his hands and knees. Ki cocked his right leg and took aim at the man's vulnerable stomach, but before he triggered his right foot, the intruder grabbed his left leg and jerked him to the ground.

The intruder tried to wrap his strong arms around Ki, but the *ninja* was too quick and darted toward the chair by the door. Grabbing his *tanto* from the chair, Ki freed its shining curved blade from the lacquered sheath. As he drew back his arm to slice at the intruder's gut, he saw the man jump to his feet and smile.

"You must be Ki," the intruder heaved, as he pulled back the duster from over his chest.

Ki's arm started in a deadly arc for the man's chest.

"Stop!" yelled Jessie. "He's wearing a badge, Ki!"

The shiny blade halted not two inches from the equally

shiny badge on the man's chest. For a moment there was a strange silence about the room as the two combatants studied each other. Ki took in the intruder's spare six-foot frame, his sun-streaked brown hair that spilled from his head over his collar, his tanned complexion, and his dark eyes that failed to show an ounce of fear in spite of the curved blade at his chest. Ki was angered at the sheepish grin on the man's face.

"You're as good as they said, Ki," the intruder said, bending to pick up his hat.

"As good as who said?" Jessie asked as she shut the door.

"As good as the governor of Texas said, for one," the intruder answered. "He sent me to see you."

"Who are you?" Ki asked.

The man cocked his head as he pulled back the duster again to expose the badge on his chest. "Wade Shaw of the Texas Rangers."

Jessie motioned with the derringer for Shaw to enter the common room.

"I'd feel more welcome if you'd put that little peashooter away."

"It's hard to welcome someone who enters your house without an invitation," she replied, motioning for him to move.

Ki turned and resheathed his knife, sliding it into his waistband. He grabbed his black vest from the chair back and slid it over his shoulders as he followed Jessie and this man into the next room. If Wade Shaw caused any more trouble, Ki would be ready.

Shaw strode around the room, taking in the abundant furniture, the great fireplace, and the portrait of Jessie's mother. He turned to Jessie. "The resemblance is striking. Your mother?"

Jessie nodded as she slid her derringer back in her pocket. "I best be asking the questions for a while, Mr. Shaw."

"Sure, but call me Wade."

"Not until you answer a few questions."

"Shoot," Shaw replied, full of confidence.

Ki thought him disrespectful of Jessie and didn't like him for it. "What's your business?" Ki blurted out.

Jessie held up her hand to silence Ki.

Ki clenched his jaw in obedient anger.

"Now, Mr. Shaw," Jessie began, "most people who come to visit us knock at the door rather than inviting themselves in."

"Yes, ma'am, I reckon that's so, but I didn't want to make any more noise than I had to and . . ." Shaw let his sentence hang as he focused his eyes on Ki.

"And?" asked Jessie.

"And I wanted to see if I could slip up on Ki there. I'd slipped up on Injuns before, but never on a *ninja,* which the best I can figure is just Injun spelled backwards."

Ki felt his anger simmering, but he knew he had to hold himself emotionless so Wade Shaw could not read his anger. Some men were more challenging to a disciplined mind than others. Wade Shaw was one of those challenges.

"Now you didn't come all the way out here just for that," Jessie said.

Shaw pursed his lips, then nodded. "The governor sent me to bring you to the capital. He has an important message for you."

Jessie shook her head. "Why didn't he telegraph me like he normally does when we've business?"

"Now, that I don't know." Shaw removed his hat and ran his fingers through his thick brown hair. "When the governor tells a Ranger to attend to matters, that's what the Ranger does, but I suspect he sent me to escort you back to the capital, serve as your bodyguard."

Ki stepped toward Shaw. "That's my job."

"And a damn good job you do," Shaw replied, drawing a giggle from Jessie as he patted the knot on the back of his head from the fall to the floor.

Ki resented Shaw for making Jessie laugh.

"I just figure the governor thought this matter was serious

enough that Miss Starbuck might need a little extra protection. Fact is, the governor pulled me off an investigation into some gun smuggling to Mexico. Seems like someone's building an army along the border to overthrow the government or invade Texas. Nobody knows for sure, but this must be mighty important for the governor to delay me getting to the bottom of the gun business."

"This is a busy season on the ranch, my favorite time of the year, Mr. Shaw, not to mention all the business I conduct from here for the Starbuck empire."

"Us Rangers always get our man or, in this case, our woman, Miss Starbuck." The cockiness that had marked his gaze and his previous words drained away from his face. "All I know for certain, Miss Starbuck, is that the governor thinks this is a life-and-death matter too delicate to be transmitted by telegraph."

Ki stepped toward Shaw. "Life and death for who?"

Shaw grimaced and offered up a slight nod. "The two of you."

"We've defended ourselves against many who have had ill will toward us," Ki answered.

Jessie agreed. "Being the daughter of Alexander Starbuck brings with it an acceptance of danger."

"So does being a Texas Ranger, but that don't mean I'm invincible."

"You're not invincible, let me assure you," Ki answered, relishing the thought that the Ranger might try to make a move for him. Ki could show Shaw just how vulnerable he was to a true warrior.

Shaw turned from Ki to Jessie. "I came here in the night, wore black to reduce the chances of being seen. The governor thinks it's important I spirit you away from here so no one knows where you are, at least for the time being."

Jessie nodded. "You'll have your answer in the morning."

"Thank you, ma'am," Shaw said. "Now, point me to the barn and I'll stay the night there until you decide."

"No," Jessie replied, "we've plenty of room in the house

14

and the night's likely to be chilly." Jessie turned to Ki. "I'll be okay, Ki, if you want to retire. I'll see you in the morning."

Ki wanted to argue and insist on staying, but he had seen the glint in Jessie's green eyes and he knew she had taken a fondness to Wade Shaw. He turned and left the room, clenching his teeth at Shaw's words.

"A real pleasure meeting you, Ki. You're as good as they say and just about as good as me."

Jessie shook her head. She liked Shaw's looks and found herself strangely attracted by his confidence, which bordered on cockiness. "You shouldn't be so sure of yourself," she chided.

The Ranger answered with a slight grin. "Got no one else to be sure of. Even the governor can be wrong."

Jessie cocked her head. "How's that?"

Shaw just smiled, taking in Jessie's fine figure, his gaze lingering on her full breasts for a moment. "The governor said you were a fine-looking woman, but he didn't say you were the prettiest thing in all of Texas."

Jessie felt a flush on her cheeks. It had been a while since a man had had this kind of effect on her. She liked it.

"Now, ma'am, if you'll just steer me to bed, I'll work out the aches from a long ride and from a hard fall on your floor." Shaw gingerly felt the back of his head for the knot Ki had given him in their brief encounter.

Easing from lamp to lamp, Jessie blew each out, then pointed to the lit stairway that led up to the bedrooms and the bath. "Care for a bath to soak out those aches? My housekeeper has drawn water in my tub."

Shaw shook his head. "I'd hate to deprive you of your bath, ma'am."

"Stop calling me 'ma'am' because the name's Jessie. And who said I'd be deprived of my bath? Not me."

At the head of the stairs, she pointed Shaw to the bathroom

door. At first he seemed not to understand what she had in mind, or perhaps he didn't want to appear too anxious. Perhaps he was just tired. As he opened the door, a cloud of warm vapor escaped into the hallway. Jessie followed him inside, pushing him toward a dressing stool and closing the door behind her. The housekeeper had heated plenty of water for the big tub in the middle of the toasty warm room. Wade Shaw removed his gunbelt, rebuckled it, and hung it over the doorknob.

"I'll help you get your boots off," she said as he sat down on the stool and stretched his legs. Her back to him, she straddled his right leg and gently tugged his boot off and tossed it to the floor. Then she straddled his left leg and started to pull on that boot, but it was stubborn and didn't give nearly as easily as the other.

Then she felt his socked right foot pushing upon her buttocks, and realized he had locked his ankle to keep the boot in place until he could assist. As he pushed against her firm bottom, he relaxed his ankle and the boot slid off. She dropped it on the floor and turned around. "My turn," she said, grabbing his hands and pulling him up.

She quickly took his place on the stool and lifted her right boot to him. He straddled her leg and slowly slid the boot from her delicate foot. For a moment he stood massaging her foot, and when he let go, she let her leg slide down the inside of his thigh. As he picked up her other leg, she lifted her bare right foot and pushed against his firm bottom. The boot slid off easily and Wade Shaw turned around, his dark eyes filled with anticipation.

"Why don't you get those dirty clothes off?" she asked.

He nodded and leisurely unbuttoned his shirt, taking his time as if to tease Jessie as much as she teased him. He let his shirt fall to the floor, and Jessie studied the downy brown hair of his muscled chest. Next, he unbuttoned his britches and let them slide down his slender legs.

Jessie licked her lips at what she saw, and he seemed pleased. Slowly, she stood and stepped toward him.

16

He held up his hand and shook his head. "Now," he said, "it's your turn."

Jessie's delicate fingers worked their way down the buttons on her workshirt. Then she unbuttoned her jeans and bent to work them down her long legs. She stepped out of her pants and straightened, then tossed her blond mane, her breasts peeking from behind her open shirt.

Shaw's eyes filled with longing, and he wiped his lips with the back of his hand as he watched for the next appearance of her breasts.

Jessie advanced another step toward him and with a sudden jerk of her arms pulled her blouse off, her firm, high breasts within his reach.

And yet he just watched, his lips widening into an inviting smile.

She let her gaze fall from his eyes to his waist, and thrilled at the excitement rising within him. She inched toward him and let her fingers brush against his throbbing manliness. He shuddered at her touch, then reached for her and pulled her flushed breasts against his chest. Jessie felt his hand slide down her back to her buttocks, then retrace its route up to her neck. His hand pressed against her blond hair and pulled her lips to his. Their lips met gently at first, then harder, like his desire, as he pulled her against him.

Jessie moaned as he stroked her hair, then let his kisses trace the curve of her jaw down the front of her neck toward her breasts. She gasped as his firm hands slid gently over her breasts, and she cried out in ecstasy as his tongue circled the brown rosebud at the tip of each. She longed for him to take each breast in his mouth, but instead he merely teased her by blowing softly across each fleshy mound.

Unable to take it anymore, she pushed him away and dropped to her knees, kneading his desire, then taking him in her mouth. She heard him moan as she gently slid her lips up and down. His hands fell to her hair, which he caressed gently as she increased her rhythm. Then he pushed her head away. Jessie looked up into his lusting eyes.

Shaw smiled at her. "I thought we came up here for a bath." He slid his powerful arm under her shoulders, then bent to slip his other arm beneath her knees. Lifting her from the floor, he carried her to the tub, gently lowering her into the water.

The warm water felt good around Jessie, but not nearly as good as Shaw's powerful but patient touch. He slipped in the tub behind her, his legs straddling her buttocks and sliding along beside her legs. His arm worked its way under her shoulder and across her breasts, gently pulling her toward him, her back coming to rest upon his strong chest. With his free hand, he twisted her head toward his and let his lips fall against hers. Jessie answered his passion with her own as both of his hands found their way to her breasts.

Now Jessie felt the excitement rising within her, a fire that needed quenching, and again Wade Shaw merely stoked that desire, instead of letting it spend itself in one flaming moment. He turned his head away from her lips and let his hands fall from her breasts. He found the soap and began to lather his hands.

"A bath, remember," he whispered into her ear as his soapy hands began to caress her soft skin and wash away the film of dust from her day's work. Shaw washed her back, her arms, and her legs hurriedly, then took his time bathing her breasts, her firm buttocks, and the triangle of fur below her waist.

Jessie relished his touch and, most of all, his patience. As frustrating as it was for satisfying her immediate desires, she knew his patience would ultimately bring even greater satisfaction. Jessie bent forward and ducked her head under the water to wet her hair. As soon as she lifted her head, his soapy hands were upon her hair, gently massaging away the dust of the day.

When he finished, Jessie rinsed her hair, then turned around to bathe him. He slid back in the tub, his arms hanging over the side as she soaped his chest and washed his legs, her hands lingering and stroking his still-firm

18

manhood. She lathered his hair and then rinsed him off, ever excited by the occasional brush of his hand against her breasts.

"Best bath I ever had," he said as he arose and helped her from the tub. He grabbed a towel and began to dry her chest and back, then her buttocks and legs. He draped the towel over her head so she could dry her hair, then grabbed another towel to dry himself off.

Jessie tossed her towel away and ran a brush through her damp hair as she watched Shaw towel off, his desire as hard as before. Shaw used his fingers for a comb on his own wet hair.

"I best put you to bed before you catch a chill," he said, scooping her up in his arms.

Jessie thrilled at the suddenness of his move, and lowered her hand to open the door, the task made difficult by his gunbelt still hanging from the knob. After she managed to open it, Shaw carried her naked into the hallway.

Jessie pointed to her bedroom. "That door," she whispered as she nuzzled against his chest.

Shaw carried her easily down the hall, pushed open the door, and proceeded straight to her bed. Reaching down, Jessie jerked the quilts and sheets back from pillows atop the feather mattress, and Shaw placed her gently in the bed. Jessie's skin prickled from the chill of the crisp, clean sheets and from the excitement of Shaw crawling in beside her. He pulled the covers over them both and began to rub her flat stomach, moving in ever-widening circles until he brushed against the edges of her full breasts and the border of that fuzzy triangle between her legs.

The sheets quickly warmed from their passion. Shaw's hands massaged her breasts, gently at first, then firmly. When he moved his hands away, Jessie closed her eyes in anticipation as his mouth found one breast, then the other. She arched her back to meet his kisses, then gasped as one of his hands found the burning spot between her legs. She rose to meet him and bucked against his touch, but he responded by lifting his hand from her womanhood and his mouth from her breasts.

Jessie hated him for his teasing game, yet loved every minute of it. She moaned in frustration, then went limp on the bed. Instantly, his hand was exploring between her legs and his mouth was suckling at her breasts. She gasped, then grabbed for him, pulling his head toward her lips.

"Now," she gasped.

Sliding his hand under her neck, he lifted Jessie's head and pressed his lips to hers as he mounted her, his legs sliding between her, his chest crushing her breasts.

Jessie lifted her hips to meet his desire. She caught her breath as he slid into her. She bucked her hips against him, desperate for him to thrust against her soft inner flesh, but he withdrew far enough to let her know he would control the pace. When she relaxed, he pushed himself against her, slowly, methodically at first. Gradually, he picked up the pace until Jessie flamed with desire.

She spread her legs as far as they would go to welcome his thrusts, then wrapped her legs around his, providing even more pleasurable leverage with each thrust. The flame of desire raged through Jessie now, and she lost track of time as Shaw's pace accelerated. She pushed up to meet him, and felt waves of pleasure surge through her body as he convulsed against her in one final, pulsating quiver of desire. Jessie gasped with satisfaction and he moaned softly with a pleasure of his own, then rolled off her, their bodies wet from perspiration and the moisture of spent passion.

Jessie cuddled up against him, resting her head on his shoulder and running her fingers through the brown hair of his muscled and heaving chest. "Now," she whispered, "it's my turn to treat you."

"You figure I've got it coming?" he asked.

"I know you do," Jessie purred, "because I'm still trembling from your touch."

Shaw ran his fingers through her hair. "You coming to the capital with me?"

20

"How could I turn down such an invitation?"

"Good," Shaw answered. "Now all I've got to do is figure out a way to get you there quick and safely."

"All you've got to do is ask me for help. I've a private Pullman on loan from the manufacturer. It's on one of the Circle Star sidings. All I've got to do is let the railroad know tomorrow and they'll add it on to the next train to the capital."

"That would work," he replied.

Jessie began to stroke his chest, gradually working her way toward his spent manhood. "The Pullman has fine sleeping quarters and an adequate bath. Of course, you'd have to guard me along the way."

"My pleasure," answered Shaw as Jessie grabbed him.

"No," Jessie replied, "the pleasure's all mine."

★

Chapter 3

Jessie could not help but be amused every time she saw the governor. He was a solid politician and a capable administrator, but he stood only five feet, two inches tall. For such a big state he was a small governor, with unruly white hair and muttonchop sideburns that dominated owl-like eyes made bigger by the thick spectacles that rested on the bridge of his abundant nose. He was now sitting behind a huge desk that swallowed up his diminutive figure, and glanced up from a stack of papers he was perusing.

He squinted over the tops of his spectacles. "I thought I left word not to be disturbed," he said in the instant before recognizing Wade Shaw, then Jessica Starbuck and Ki. "My apologies," he said, jumping out of his chair and straightening his frock coat and string tie as he scurried around the desk. "I didn't expect you back so quickly, Wade."

The Texas Ranger nodded. "The railroad hooked Miss Starbuck's private Pullman onto the next train and we made good time."

The governor smiled at Jessie, then took her hand and patted it as he would a child's. "Good to see you, Jessie, and I do appreciate you coming here, especially under such odd circumstances."

Jessie smiled at the governor's paternal manner, and stifled a giggle at his unstately stature.

He released her hand and motioned toward a circle of plush chairs around a polished table. "I trust you had a good journey?" he offered.

Wade Shaw answered before Jessie could respond. "Very satisfying trip," he said. "Most satisfying I've ever had." The Ranger winked over the governor's head at Jessie.

Jessie answered Shaw with a knowing look, then turned to the governor. "A good trip, though I've had better." She tossed a smile of gentle retribution toward Shaw. "You remember Ki, Governor, do you not?"

Ki stood sullenly nearby. Ki had not taken to Wade Shaw, nor to him sharing Jessie's sleeping berth on the trip from the Circle Star.

"Yes, indeed," the governor said, reaching to shake Ki's hand.

Ki gave the governor a firm handshake. "Good to again see you."

The governor motioned to a chair for Jessie. Ki scurried to the seat at her side before Wade Shaw could claim it.

"Fastest I've seen you move since the night we met," Shaw offered as he strode to a chair across the table.

Jessie eased delicately into the overstuffed chair, and then the governor took a seat on her other side.

The politician leaned forward in his chair and drummed his fingers on the high gloss of the polished table. "I apologize for summoning you here this way, Jessie."

"We know you are a cautious man who wouldn't call us without reason. We stand to serve you and the state any way that we can."

The governor's hand folded into a tiny fist and he hit the table once. "I'm honored by your comments. This state owes you a great debt for all you have done in the name of justice. The work you and Ki have done, not just in virtually wiping out the cartel, but also in righting wrongs wherever you found them, can never be fully rewarded."

23

"My father taught me well, Governor, and left me the business and financial resources to do something about injustice. That and Ki made it all possible for me."

Ki gave a slight nod of acknowledgment.

"I agree," Wade Shaw interjected. "Ki's a hell of a fighter."

"Now, Governor," Jessie said, "what brought us to the capital?"

The governor drummed his fingers on the table as he started to talk. "It's your safety," the governor began. "We've gotten word, actually Ranger Shaw here found out about it, that an international assassin called 'The Scorpion' has been dispatched from Europe to Texas with the sole purpose of killing you and Ki."

Jessie let her mind run free, trying to recollect if she had ever heard of The Scorpion. She looked at Ki, and he answered with an almost imperceptible shrug as he leaned forward in his chair. Jessie could recall no cartel assassin of that name and doubted any connection.

"The Scorpion has more than a dozen victims that we know of in Europe, but no one knows what he looks like, much less who he is," the governor continued. "He's a shrewd and successful assassin, likely made more so since the general demise of the cartel."

Jessie pursed her lips as she thought of any fragment of a clue she might remember. "I've feared the virtual elimination of the cartel would lead to this. With the absence of an effective cartel, a vacuum has been created in the global underworld. With any vacuum, it's only a matter of time until it is filled. The unscrupulous would naturally want to take over where the cartel left off."

Wade Shaw leaned over the table and propped his elbows on the polished wood. "That might explain rumors I'm investigating, Jessie, that somebody was bankrolling gun purchases for Mexico to foment a rebellion that might overflow into Texas and the rest of the United States. There's great evil out there if you look below the surface."

24

The governor nodded. "Wade came across word of The Scorpion in his investigation. The gun smuggling can present serious problems for this state and the United States, but I felt this rumor of The Scorpion had even more significant ramifications, knowing your resources and the influence of the Starbuck empire. Frankly, Jessie, I'm worried for your safety."

Ki cleared his throat, and Jessie thought she saw the first trace of a grin to cross Ki's lips since he left the Circle Star.

"And your safety too, Ki," the governor immediately answered.

Jessie smiled. "No, Governor, I think he meant that he had successfully protected me against the cartel and he would do it against The Scorpion."

Ki nodded.

The governor shook his head. "Even so, and with no disrespect to you, Ki, I feel obliged to offer you protection until The Scorpion is found and crushed by the might of the Texas Rangers."

Ki scowled across the table at Wade Shaw, who just smirked proudly back.

"Governor," Jessie replied, "with all due respect to Wade Shaw, who I know can be a hard-driving law officer, I feel we are capable of taking care of ourselves against whatever The Scorpion can throw against us. Ki is trained in *ninjutsu*, the art of the *ninja*. His mastery of the martial arts and Eastern ways and his single-minded devotion to my safety have protected me against enemies of far greater danger and with far bigger reputations than The Scorpion."

Ki cocked his head and smirked at Wade Shaw.

The governor stood up from his chair, stretching himself to his full height, then strutting about the room like a sick rooster. "I feared you would refuse my offer."

"Then why did you call us to the capital if you expected our refusal?" Jessie asked.

"Politics being politics, Jessie, I could not afford to learn

25

of this plot and not inform you. Why, if something were to happen to you and word leaked out I had known about it in advance, it could cost me the next election."

"We wouldn't want that, now would we, Governor?" Ki responded.

Jessie shot him a disapproving glance. "This is my favorite time of the year on the ranch, Governor. I don't think you should worry about us there."

The governor ran his fingers through his white hair. "That's just the problem. That's the place The Scorpion would look first. I figure you need to be someplace else, somewhere that The Scorpion might not so readily expect you."

Wade Shaw grinned as he looked at Ki. "You could always have me arrest them and keep them under protective custody, Governor."

Ki snarled, "We'd be safer without the Rangers than with them. They know nothing of the true arts of combat and disguise. All they know is gunpowder and fists."

Wade Shaw stroked his chin, then pointed at the badge on his chest. "Us Rangers wear our stars instead of throwing them like you do."

"The *shuriken* is a silent weapon, just like the *ninja,*" Ki shot back. "You Rangers make a lot of noise like your guns. My actions—not my noise—speak for me."

"Gentlemen, gentlemen." The governor threw up his hands in exasperation and marched behind his desk. He stood for a moment at the window, staring out toward tall trees with their budding leaves. "I don't want you fighting each other. It's The Scorpion we should be worried about."

Jessie nodded. "The governor is right about that, though wrong, I fear, on what is best for our safety. Ki has been a noble protector for many years. I am safe with him."

Wade Shaw leaned across the table toward her. "I think what the governor is saying is that we should take no chances. Perhaps it's wise to return to the ranch and go about your business, but just perhaps it is wiser to make people think you are at the Circle Star. That would throw The Scorpion off your tail for a while, and maybe buy us a little more time to find out who he is and take care of him." Wade paused a moment and stared at Ki. "Ki's reputation as a bodyguard is superb. Nobody, myself included, questions that, though I admit I've had a little fun jawing at him. We're all just trying to do what's best for you."

Jessie let out a slow breath and tossed her head. "The flaw in your logic, Wade, is that people already know we are in the capital. My Pullman can't leave the Circle Star siding without people knowing I've left and knowing I've arrived once I get wherever I'm going."

Ki folded his hands on the table. "She is correct."

The Ranger shrugged at Ki. "And that works to our advantage in this instance." Shaw turned to Jessie. "You've got businesses all over the country, several places where you could wait out the next week or so."

"True," Jessie responded, "but no place I'd rather be than on the ranch. And I don't care to be run off from my own place by a mere threat of something we don't know for fact." She leaned back in her overstuffed chair and awaited Shaw's response.

"There'll be other springtimes on your ranch, Jessie, as long as you and The Scorpion don't cross paths," Wade answered.

Ki patted his hand on the table. "The Scorpion might not survive an encounter with us. Many others bent on our destruction haven't."

Wade Shaw let out a slow breath of exasperation, then pushed his chair away from the table and stood up, unfolding his long frame and shaking his head. "All I want is time. We'll board you on your Pullman this afternoon before sundown so everyone'll see. We'll start you back for the Circle Star after dark. Then at the Colorado River crossing, your train'll stop to let a freight train cross the bridge. We slip you off the Pullman and spirit you someplace else. Then everyone will still think you've gone back to the ranch, and then you can leave the state for a while."

Jessie shook her head. "No! I'll not be run from Texas, just on some rumor about some unknown assassin named for a . . . a bug." Jessie crossed her arms beneath her bosom and felt Shaw's covetous gaze upon her blouse. She admired his persistence and his concern, but she would not be driven from Texas. Neither would she find unnecessary work to attend to in another state until this threat, if it existed at all, was thwarted. Of course, there was that invitation from the English industrialist Lord Clinton Bly to meet in Galveston to discuss items of mutual interest. She hadn't yet telegraphed a response to his invitation.

"Will you agree to go into hiding for a week, no more?" Shaw asked.

Turning away from the window, the governor ran his fingers through his hair. "Please, Jessie, for your own good."

And for the good of the governor's next election, Jessie thought. Even if the governor was worried about The Scorpion's implications for his next election, Jessie couldn't hold it against him. He was at least honest enough to admit it. She'd take honesty from a politician in any dose she could get, the species being only slightly more respected than the brotherhood of thieves.

"I'll agree not to return to the Circle Star," Jessie offered, "but I . . ."

A smile worked its way across the governor's face, but disappeared the instant Ki shot up from his chair.

"You don't have to do this. I can protect you," Ki protested with a wave of his arm.

Before Jessie could respond, Wade Shaw answered. "Nobody in this room thinks otherwise, Ki. It's just that we want to take all the precautions we can. As a *ninja* you wouldn't take risks you don't have to take. Same thing here."

"Gentlemen," Jessie resumed, "I had not finished."

All eyes turned toward Jessie.

"I'll agree not to return to the Circle Star, if it will accommodate the fears of the governor and the Texas

Rangers, but only because I have business I can conduct elsewhere in the state."

"Where?" Wade Shaw asked.

"Galveston."

"Why, hell, Jessie, you being in Galveston would be secret for five minutes before everyone in the state would know about it. You and I know Galveston is as busy a place as there is in the state, all the shipping and commerce there."

Jessie shook her finger at the Ranger. "I've never run away from trouble and I'll not start now, Wade Shaw."

"But why Galveston, Jessie?"

"It's Galveston or the Circle Star, Wade Shaw."

"But why?"

"I have an invitation to meet Lord Clinton Bly," she replied.

The governor's glance shot to Jessie. "Lord Clinton Bly, the English textiles mogul?"

Jessie nodded. "I had planned to turn down his invitation, to stay on the ranch and work the spring branding. Fact, I planned to telegraph him my regrets until Wade Shaw convinced me to come to the capital without delay."

The governor shook his head in disbelief. "You'd turn down an invitation with Lord Clinton Bly to brand cattle?"

Jessie ignored the governor's question, staring instead at Wade Shaw. "It's Galveston or the Circle Star, one or the other."

The governor scurried to Jessie. "By all means, go to Galveston. We should not snub Lord Clinton Bly. After all, he has money to invest in Texas."

Shaw cleared his throat. "What about Jessie's safety?"

"Of course, Wade, of course," the governor replied. "I'll assign you to accompany them and keep and eye on things."

"We don't need him for a nursemaid," Ki offered, then crossed his arms over his chest.

"Looks like you'll have me anyway, Ki," Shaw answered. "Governor's orders."

Jessie smiled at the thought of Wade Shaw as an escort, but Ki only scowled.

29

★

Chapter 4

The sun was a low flame burning on the horizon beyond the
capital. Slowly lamps were being lit and the city was taking
on the speckled pallor of lamplight. Though it was not the
busiest time of the day, the train station was still abuzz
with activity as night approached. The westbound passenger
train impatiently hissed and huffed as it was delayed long
enough for a special Pullman car to be coupled to the back.
The conductor stood impatiently on the passenger platform,
tapping his foot on the wood and staring at his pocket watch.

Spectators on the platform pointed and gossiped as the
Pullman was shoved into the rear of the train, the jar of the
coupling reverberating down the line of cars to the locomotive,
which sent a plume of smoke in the air. Cinders made the trail
of smoke glow softly above the growl of the locomotive. Men,
women, and children inside the passenger cars opened their
windows and stuck their heads out to see if they could glimpse
what was causing the delay.

No sooner had the Pullman been coupled with the train
than a carriage with drawn curtains drew up beside the
platform.

"Look," shouted a young boy, "it's the governor's coach."

All heads turned toward the carriage, and the murmuring picked up as everyone admired the governor's well-apportioned rig and the matched gray geldings that pulled it. When the door swung open, a lean Texas Ranger emerged and the spectators hushed, several on the platform moving toward the coach for a glimpse of the governor himself. A couple of men laughed, pleased that they would finally get a chance to see for themselves if the governor was as short as everyone said.

The Ranger stood beside the door and offered his hand to a striking woman with a statuesque figure and honey-blond hair that fell well past her shoulders. It wasn't the governor, but it wasn't bad either, several men agreed as they took in Jessica Starbuck's full bosom, her narrow waist, and her rounded bottom. In the dying light of day, her beauty seemed to shine as a light of its own. Taking the hand of Wade Shaw, Jessie stepped from the coach and toward the ball of light from a nearby gas lamp. In the light she straightened the lapels of her green tweed riding jack, then brushed her hand against the pleats of her matching skirt. The soft white of her silk blouse accentuated the glow of her flawless face. To the surprise of the male spectators, this beautiful woman wore a holster and revolver on her shapely hips.

Next the Ranger offered his hand to a muscled man who, like himself, stood over six feet tall. The man had long black hair with pencil-thin eyebrows and mustache. The man seemed disgusted with the Ranger's outstretched hand. As he shook his head to reject it, Ki jumped from the coach, landing with the grace of a panther. He wore a blue-gray tweed suit over a sky-blue shirt and a black vest. Around his neck he wore a string tie, and on his feet rode ankle-high Wellington boots.

The Ranger closed the coach door, and several men shook their heads in admiration of Jessie, though no one had recognized her. "Don't guess the governor accompanied the young lady," said one man.

"The governor's dumber than I thought," replied another.

The Ranger escorted Jessie and Ki up the platform, then

31

toward the Pullman. The conductor, disgusted that anyone would cause a delay in his precious schedule, hesitated to offer assistance, then realized he should, and scurried toward the private car. By the time he reached the Pullman, the Ranger had already helped them inside.

Wade Shaw stepped down from the Pullman just as the conductor arrived, still holding his watch in one hand. Wade Shaw grabbed the conductor by the arm and turned him around.

"Huh?" the conductor asked, taken by surprise. "You realize this delay has put us behind schedule. The evening freight will beat us to the river bridge and delay us further."

Wade Shaw shrugged. "The evening freight'll pass first tonight unless you want to argue with the president of the company."

The conductor gulped, his Adam's apple bobbing nervously.

Wade Shaw threw his arm around the conductor's shoulders and started the railroad man back down the platform in the direction from which he had come. When Shaw was beneath passenger windows where he was certain others could hear, he spoke again to the conductor. "Do you know who that was that just got on the train?"

Shaking his head, the conductor said, "I hear that Pullman belongs to a wealthy rancher, but I can't say for certain."

The Ranger nodded, then spoke loudly so others couldn't help but hear. "Yes, sir, that was Jessica Starbuck, perhaps the world's richest woman, and her assistant, Ki."

"That don't give her the right to delay this train."

Shaw figured he'd take a little vinegar out of the conductor with his next remark, even though he was uncertain whether it was true. "Yes, sir, maybe you are right, but I don't know that I'd be saying that to many people, Miss Starbuck being one of the major stockholders in your railroad."

The conductor gulped again and his shoulders sagged beneath Shaw's arm. "Maybe I spoke too hastily."

Shaw decided to give the conductor a final worry. "I wouldn't tell a soul that you insulted a major stockholder," he said, a little louder than was necessary. "I just hope nobody overheard your insult of Miss Starbuck." Shaw looked around at the passengers beginning to pull their heads back inside the car windows and at the spectators still lingering on the platform. He saw that several were talking, no doubt about Jessica Starbuck, and knew that word would get around the capital. There might even be a newspaper mention in a day or two of her capital visit and her return to the Starbuck ranch. That would buy him and the Texas Rangers a little more time to identify The Scorpion, provided Jessica didn't make too big a splash in Galveston. That still worried him.

But he was not nearly as worried as the conductor, whose hand with the watch had drooped to his side. From the look on his face, the conductor was seeing his years of service and his retirement nest egg slipping away like seconds on his railroad timepiece. "Perhaps there are some things I can do to assist Miss Starbuck."

"Yes, sir, there is," Shaw answered. "She's a very private person with a lot of business to attend to. Do not disturb her or enter her Pullman unless requested to do so by her assistant or myself. She's food enough to last until she gets to the Circle Star Ranch. If we need something, we'll find you on board."

"Yes, sir," the conductor answered, "whatever you think best."

"It's not just me that thinks it best," Wade Shaw replied, deciding to give the conductor a full dose, "but the governor and the Texas Rangers as well." Shaw removed his arm from the conductor's shoulder. "I best be joining Miss Starbuck."

He left the conductor dazed behind him and strode back down the platform to the Pullman. He bounded up the steps and inside, knowing something the conductor didn't. It would be another fifteen, maybe twenty minutes before the train pulled away from the platform. That would ensure that the freight train would beat this one to the river bridge, where they would slip off the back of the Pullman and return by a buggy to the station for a Galveston-bound train.

When Wade Shaw entered the Pullman, he laughed. "We've got ourselves a nervous conductor now. He was complaining about the delay, and I told him you were a major stockholder in the railroad company."

Jessica offered him a soft smile and a nod. "I am!"

Shaw seemed surprised. "Is there anything you don't own?"

"The Texas Rangers," she answered.

"Here's one you could own." Shaw looked toward the back of the Pullman and Jessie's sleeping berth. A sly grin slid across his face as he thought of the trip from the Circle Star to the capital.

Jessica smiled back, as if considering the offer.

"You don't have time," Ki told them.

Wade Shaw nodded. "It was a pleasant thought."

"How do we know," Ki asked sarcastically, "that *you* aren't The Scorpion?"

Shaw felt anger rising in him. Why the hell was Ki always baiting him? Was Ki jealous that he had slept with Jessie? Was Ki trying to drive a wedge between him and Jessie? My, but she was a fine woman, an exciting woman, one who would arouse any man. Shaw wondered why Ki was so circumspect around her, so protective of her. Ki was almost a mother hen to Jessie. Shaw stared into Ki's dark eyes and could feel the *ninja's* suspicions. He thought it best to ignore the question. He settled into a thick leather-cushioned seat opposite Jessie.

Receiving no answer, Ki spoke again. "How do we know you aren't The Scorpion? You broke into the ranch house to find us. What's to say you wouldn't have killed us had I not heard your bumbling approach?"

Jessie slapped her hands together. "You two, hush up! I'm tired of you being at each other's throats all the time."

Finally, the locomotive began to whistle, then lurch forward, the clang of the couplings ringing out down the line like a roll call among cars. The Pullman jerked ahead, then began to accelerate, gradually leaving the station and passing the city's houses and buildings, none nearly as impressive as the capitol itself.

At the edge of the city, Wade began to kill the lamps in the Pullman so no one from outside could see them or—if The Scorpion was around—take a sniper's shot at them.

The three rode in silence until the measured click of the train over the track slowed and the cars followed the locomotive onto a siding that approached the river bridge.

Ki stood up, ready to exit.

"Wait, Ki," Shaw ordered. "We don't leave until the freight train has passed and we start to moving again. It'll reduce the risk of us being seen in the freight train's headlights or by passengers on this train looking around."

When Ki sat silently down, Wade knew his logic had made sense.

In a few minutes, the freight train rumbled past, its headlight throwing a brief glow inside the darkened car. Shaw caught a glimpse of Jessie, and she seemed to smile at him. After the freight train passed, the passenger train began to inch forward.

"Now it's time for us to go," the Ranger ordered.

Ki jumped from his seat and led Jessie and Shaw out the back of the Pullman. Ki jumped off the back of the car as it inched toward the bridge. Then Shaw stepped down and walked alongside the car to help Jessie. She jumped into his arms, and he felt her breasts against his chest and her breath upon his neck. It was a good feeling until Ki stepped over to them.

"Where's the wagon?" Ki asked. "We must return to the station."

Ki knew where the wagon was because he could see it in the trees. Shaw had been wise to kill the Pullman lamps as they left town, but not just for the reasons he likely had. Knowing the way Rangers reasoned, Ki figured Shaw had

35

turned out the lights so they would be less easily visible. The real advantage to killing the lamps was that it allowed time for the eyes to adjust to the darkness and see things much more readily.

As Ki scanned the area, he used his off-center vision, a skill he had honed through the years. Rather than stare right at an object he was focusing on, as he did in daylight, he had learned to look five to ten degrees away from the object in darkness. Odd though it seemed, and difficult as it was to explain, this made the object become better focused in the darkness. He had learned to scan vast expanses of ground in the same way, by moving his gaze in short, irregular intervals over an area without directly staring at it.

That was how he had spotted the buggy with the man seated atop it and a horse tied behind. As a *ninja* he knew that the eye spots movement first, then silhouette, and finally color. Color was eliminated in the dark, so a man had only movement and silhouette to look for with his off-center vision. First Ki had seen the movement of the man twisting in the buggy, then the silhouette.

"The wagon's supposed to be here," Shaw offered.

"Then show me," Ki demanded.

Shaw released his hold on Jessie and turned to look. By his long pause, Ki knew Shaw had not yet spotted the buggy.

Ki lifted his hand and pointed his finger at the buggy. "Could that be it?" he asked, knowing full well it was.

Shaw followed the direction of Ki's hand, and grumbled that Ki had spotted it first.

Ki crossed his arms over his chest. "How do you know that's not The Scorpion in the buggy?"

Ignoring the question, Shaw cut loose a shrill whistle. His whistle was answered by two sharp whistles. "It's one of my men, here where he was supposed to be." The buggy made a tight circle and emerged from the trees and onto the railroad's cleared right-of-way.

The new Ranger drew the buggy up beside Wade Shaw.

"You're running a bit late, Wade. Think you have time to make the train?"

"We won't push it too fast," Shaw answered. "I don't want to draw attention to us, but I don't want the train to leave without us either."

Ki shook his head. The Ranger didn't have this planned as well as he should have. Wade Shaw could never make a *ninja* because he didn't see far enough beyond his own face to learn the true patience and thought that the master of the martial arts required.

Shaw issued instructions to his man. "You ride ahead and hold the southbound train until we get there."

The second Ranger nodded, then tied the reins and jumped out of the buggy. As Wade Shaw helped Jessie into the buggy seat, the other Ranger mounted the spare horse and galloped off toward town.

Wade Shaw turned to Ki. "There's not enough room in the seat for the three of us. You'll have to ride in the back."

"You can ride in the back yourself, Wade Shaw."

Jessie interrupted, impatience in her voice. "Why do you two persist in fussing?"

Wade Shaw laughed. "Because we like each other so."

"Wade's familiar with the roads, Ki, so let him drive."

Ki knew Jessie was correct, but certainly wasn't going to give any visible sign he agreed. He said nothing, but jumped in the back of the wagon before Wade could climb aboard. "Are we sitting here until dawn or is Wade Shaw going to take us back to town."

The Ranger grumbled as he climbed into the buggy and dropped his muscled frame into the seat. Quickly he untied the reins. "Hiya," he yelled as he aimed the buggy toward the lights flickering in the distance.

"Don't you worry," he said to Jessie, "we'll make it there in time for you to slip onto the train without anyone knowing."

Jessie shook her head. "You've been more worried about my safety than I have. I've still got Ki for security."

Ki took silent glee in Jessie's remarks and her subsequent quietude. He leaned back in the buggy, enjoying as best he could the trip over the trail that rose and fell over the gentle hills outside the capital. The horse made good time, occasionally slowing as he reached the top of a hill.

At the top of one particularly high hill, the buggy came to a sudden stop as two men jumped from the adjacent trees. "Halt," they yelled simultaneously.

Then one stepped forward. "This is a holdup, mister. We want the valuables from you and your wife."

★

Chapter 5

Ki slid quietly from the back of the buggy, ever careful to move slowly without any sudden movements. The same knowledge that had helped him spot the buggy in the trees would help him slip up on the two bandits.

"Your money, mister, because my gun's pointed right at your wife."

Ki felt a surge of anger boiling through his veins that one of these bandits would threaten Jessie. This damn fool scheme of Wade Shaw's had endangered Jessie more than The Scorpion ever would. For that matter, one of these robbers could actually be The Scorpion. Ki touched the ground, his Wellington boots snapping a twig that seemed to echo throughout the hills. Ki froze just as Wade Shaw spoke.

"You fellows have made the biggest mistake of your outlaw lives," Shaw said. "I'm a Texas Ranger."

"Well," replied one of the bandits, "I'm our midget governor. Why don't you just take my orders and give me your money. Then you can be on your way, Mr. Texas Ranger, you and your wife there."

Ki crouched behind the buggy. Now he had to become invisible to his enemies as he stalked them. He wished he wore black *ninja* garb because it would make his hiding easier. Then he shrugged. His dark suit would do. These two men were ignorant of the ways of the *ninja*. For a moment Ki stayed behind the buggy. Then he circled away toward the trees, moving in uneven steps on his tiptoes, a technique known as *P'a Pu* in the *ninjutsu*. The uneven steps and the distorted body motions helped conceal his faint silhouette in the dark and decrease the chances he would be seen.

"Well, Mr. Texas Ranger," said the bandit leader, "maybe you and the missus should just get down from the wagon until we get your valuables. Just remember if you try anything smart, Barney there's keeping a gun aimed at your wife."

"Dammit, Claude, you shouldn't have mentioned my name," said the other bandit. "Oooops."

Shaw bent over and tied the reins. "Wade Shaw's my name. Pleasure to meet you, Barney, and you too, Claude. I gather you two aren't real experienced in this line of work."

"See what you did, Claude," Barney called, his voice cracking with nervousness. "You identified me."

"You did the same to me, Barney."

Ki advanced beyond the two bandits and circled back. He had to be fast. The more nervous the two grew, the more dangerous they became to Jessie. Ki would glance toward the bandits occasionally, but he never let his eyes fix on them because to stare too long would interfere with his well-developed night vision.

Shaw eased out of the buggy, then offered to help Jessie down, but Claude interrupted.

"Let the missus get out on her side so Barney can keep a better eye on her."

"Quit using my name, Claude. What if this fellow really is a Texas Ranger. Say, he may be a Ranger 'cause his wife is wearing a gunbelt and revolver!"

Ki turned and edged toward the road. He was behind the bandits now and they were at his mercy. As much as he hated to admit it, Wade Shaw had played this smoothly, never giving the hint of Ki's presence, yet stalling the bandits long enough for Ki to slip around them.

Now Ki advanced, formulating his plan with each irregular step. One hand slipped inside his coat to his vest and pulled out a *shuriken.* This he would use on the leader, who was close to Shaw. The Ranger would be on his own after Ki loosed his throwing star. Ki would attack Barney with his hands to deflect his gun from Jessie.

"Okay, Mr. Ranger," said Claude. "Empty your pockets and keep your hand away from that sidearm. One move for it and I'll shoot you and Barney'll shoot your missus."

"Dammit, Claude, quit using my name."

Ki's hand felt the cold, sharp steel of a throwing star. He pulled it from its pocket as he slipped within three paces of Barney. The horse pulling the buggy nickered. That would have been an indication of trouble to anyone who knew the martial arts, Ki thought, but these two were inept as robbers.

Wade Shaw spoke. "I carry my wallet in my boot. You want me to get it?"

"Sure," answered Claude, "slow and easy."

"It could be a knife," Barney said nervously.

Ki tiptoed within reach of Barney and saw the nervous quiver of his gun hand. He had to act quickly. He let out a slow breath of anticipation. The gelding was fidgeting now, shaking its head and rattling the harness. And the gelding stood between him and Claude, partially obstructing his view of the bandit leader. The horse would make the throw harder.

Beyond the horse, Ki saw Wade Shaw bend over and reach for his boot. Claude seemed to lean forward with him. Ki knew he had to act now. He had to throw from his shoulder and hope to strike Claude high.

The horse raised its head, then dropped it, tossing at the harness. Ki lifted his arm above his shoulder, then whipped the arm forward, snapping the wrist. The star flew from his hand and Ki immediately did a full spin toward Barney, grabbing his gun hand and ripping it upward.

Beyond the horse, Claude screamed as the *shuriken* dug into the flesh of his shoulder.

Barney cried in pain and terror as Ki grabbed his forearm and bent his gun hand back over it. When his wrist snapped, the revolver fell harmlessly to the ground and Jessie lunged to get it, picking it up and aiming it at Barney.

Ki released Barney's gun hand and it fell limp to his side. As he screamed, his other hand reached instinctively for the now-lame one. As he did, Ki clasped his fingers together, threw his hands behind Barney's neck, and with all his strength jerked the bandit's head forward. As the bandit stumbled, Ki backed up, then jerked up his knee to meet the bandit's head. Ki's knee crushed Barney's nose, then smashed savagely into his face. Instantly, Barney fell limp beside the buggy.

Without a moment's hesitation, Ki darted around the horse to assist Wade Shaw, but the Texas Ranger didn't need any help now. Claude was sprawled on the ground, groaning at the pain in his shoulder and at the bite of Shaw's boots as the Ranger stood on the would-be robber's wrists.

Shaw shook his head. "Damnedest thing I ever didn't see, Ki. I felt the buggy give when you slid out the back, but I never saw you until you attacked."

"I made myself invisible," Ki said as he bent over Claude and jerked the star from his shoulder. Claude gave a cry, then passed out as Ki wiped the star on the man's shirt. Ki then slipped the star back in his vest.

"Let's drag them out of the road so they don't get run over, then get back to town," Shaw said. "We've a train to catch." Shaw grabbed one arm and Ki the other to pull Claude into the trees.

As they dragged Barney to the opposite side of the road, Jessie climbed back in the buggy. "I'd say you two make a pretty good team."

Shaw still shook his head. "Damnedest thing I ever didn't see," he repeated as he jumped up onto the seat beside Jessie and untied the reins. "You aboard, Ki?"

"Am now," Ki answered.

Shaw slapped the reins against the horse's rump. "Hold on, you two, we've got a train to catch and time to make up. Hiya, hiya!" The horse pulled full into the harness, advancing at a trot along the trail all the way to the station.

Ki held tightly to the bouncing buggy, thinking along the way that he had gained a measure of respect from Shaw. Ki had to give the Ranger credit for not giving the robbers any indication of his presence.

Approaching the station, Ki could see the train puffing steam and smoke beside the platform. The Ranger who had ridden to town ahead of Shaw, Jessie, and Ki stood on the platform and pointed to the approaching wagon. He motioned to the engineer, and almost instantly the steam breath of the locomotive began to pick up its pace.

Shaw circled the buggy over a track crossing and then parallel to the railroad, approaching the train from the side without the platform. "Damn," Shaw said as he passed a baggage car.

"What is it, Wade?" asked Jessie.

"This is the payroll train, taking the government payroll to Houston and Galveston. Always a greater chance for trouble on the payroll runs than the regular runs."

"We'll be okay, Wade. You saw what Ki did to those two ruffians down the trail."

"Ki's a good one, a bit stubborn at times, but a good man to ride with." Shaw passed one passenger car, then reined up at the second. "Here's where you get off." He reached in his pocket and pulled out two tickets. "This'll get you and Ki to Galveston."

"What about you, Wade?" Jessie asked.

Ki heard the desire in her voice and was envious, though he could never admit that to Jessie or anyone else. He was bound to death to protect Jessie, and he could never do anything that might jeopardize his commitment to her well-being.

"There's no sleeping berths on this train, Jessie, so I figured I might just as well ride up front with the engineer."

Shaw laughed. "I figured I pleased you on the way to the capital, and I could please Ki by staying out of his sight on the way to Galveston."

Ki grimaced. Though he didn't like Shaw's smart-alecky attitude or his cavalier comment to Jessie, Ki figured Shaw could be a likable fellow if he learned to keep his mouth shut. That, however, would be pretty near impossible for the Ranger with his surplus arrogance. Ki just wished Jessie didn't enjoy his company nearly so much. He slipped out of the wagon and helped Jessie down and to the passenger car, then boarded himself as Shaw turned the buggy about and raced back down to the locomotive. The last Ki saw of him, he was climbing out of the buggy and into the steam engine.

Almost immediately, the locomotive began to inch forward, then pick up speed. Ki was glad to be shed of Wade Shaw. He stared at Jessie and saw a wistful look in her green eyes. She was sure taken by this Ranger.

The passenger car was crowded as Jessie entered. Alternating rows of seats faced each other so that some passengers rode with their backs to the front.

A rotund conductor stood in the middle of the aisle, a scowl on his face and a ticket punch in his hand. "Tickets, please," he said as the train began to gather speed.

Several people glanced over their shoulders to see who had been the last to board. Up front, two men nudged each other and pointed with approval at Jessie. They were scruffy types, with unkempt beards and bad teeth. Even in the crowded passenger car, nobody sat in the seat facing them.

One of them stood up and took off his straw hat. "Hey, girlee," he yelled, "we saved you a seat with us."

Jessie felt her stomach turn.

"But not for your damn Chink friend," called the second one.

They giggled and elbowed one another at their cleverness.

Jessie handed the tickets to the conductor.

44

"Just ignore them," the conductor offered as he punched their tickets. "They've had a bit to drink."

"I should teach them some manners," Ki offered.

"No, Ki," Jessie said. "We don't want to draw any more attention to ourselves than we have to."

The conductor returned their tickets and offered a sickly smile. "If they give you too much trouble, I'll see what I can do, but there's four more of them in the front car. I don't know if they're brothers or what, but they are as crude a bunch as I've ever seen." The conductor turned and walked to the front of the car. As he passed the two troublemakers, one of them stuck his foot in the aisle. The conductor stumbled, caught his balance, and twisted his head around to scowl at his tormentors.

The one with his straw hat tossed it on his seat and lifted his fists in front of him. "Care to take me on?" he challenged.

Shaking his head, the conductor passed out of the car without a word. Jessie saw him linger on the platform between the two cars as if he dreaded going into the next.

Jessie looked around for a pair of seats together, but saw none. Ki pointed to an aisle seat she could take and another down the aisle by the window.

Jessie heard the offers of the two scruffy men.

"Blondie, you can sit by me," called the one with the straw hat.

"Hell, you can sit in my lap," shouted the other.

They both laughed.

Around the car the other passengers tried to ignore the unruly pair, looking awkwardly away or pretending they hadn't heard anything.

Jessie took a seat that, unfortunately, faced the two troublemakers. She saw Ki nod reassuringly, letting her know he wouldn't let the men pester her long. "No, Ki," she said. "It's easier to put up with it than to create a commotion. Let's just get to Galveston quietly."

"If they will allow it. I don't like their looks. They have

45

evil intent in their eyes." Ki moved down the aisle and slid past uncomfortable passengers to get to the window seat.

After ten or fifteen minutes, the two men looked at a pocket watch, then settled meekly in their seats, their evil eyes glaring at the passengers they faced. Some passengers shut their eyes as if trying to catch some sleep, while most just looked away.

Jessie had settled into her seat, and had decided to ignore the two men the rest of the trip, when the front door opened and two more scruffy-looking men walked in. They bent over the first two, all whispering to one another, then departed back into the next car. The one in the straw hat held up his watch to the lamp and studied the time for two or three minutes.

When he finally snapped the watch cover shut, he nudged his partner. Instantly, both stood up, their hands holding drawn weapons.

"Folks," said Straw Hat, "we're robbing the train."

★

Chapter 6

Women screamed and grabbed their children while men squirmed in their seats, gauging whether to risk hiding their wallets or pulling a weapon and fighting back. Jessie glanced quickly toward Ki. She had never seen such a bewildered look upon the face of her *ninja* protector.

Ki caught Jessie's glance and just shook his head. He mouthed, "Twice in one night," then his dark eyes narrowed. He turned and stared back at the two robbers.

Though she wore her .38-caliber revolver on her hip, Jessie patted her leg for the derringer she carried in the garter holster beneath her skirt. The derringer would be easier to hide. She stared straight ahead as Straw Hat took off his headgear and began to wave it and his pistol under the noses of the folks in the seat behind his. His partner did the same on the other side of the aisle.

"Now, folks," yelled Straw Hat, "stay calm and nobody's gonna get hurt. You men folks just keep your hands up over your heads where we can see them. All we want is your valuables: wallets, watches, jewelry, gold, coins. That's a small price to pay for your lives." Straw Hat laughed.

A couple of women began to sob, and one sandy-headed girl no more than five began to squeal.

"Shut her up, woman," yelled Straw Hat, "before it gets on my nerves and I shut her up forever."

The girl's mother covered her daughter's mouth and nodded, fear overflowing in the tears at the corner of her eyes.

"Okay, folks, now pay up," Straw Hat demanded, shaking the hat in front of his first victims and alternately glancing from them to the rest of the passengers.

Jessie worked her hand down her side and began to tug her skirt up. Gradually, her hem passed her calf, then reached her knee, and continued on to mid-thigh. Jessie glanced from Straw Hat toward Ki, who held his hands up in the air. From the narrow set of his eyes to the stony scowl of his lips, Ki was merely biding his time to unleash his caged fury upon the robbers. With Ki nearby, Jessie felt confident they could disarm these two, but what about the others? The conductor had mentioned this pair's allies in the next car, so several more bandits rode the train. But why would these fellows hold up a train for the pocket change of the passengers? Then Jessie remembered Wade Shaw noting this train would be carrying a government payroll as well. Now it made sense.

Jessie slowly lifted her gaze from Ki, her eyes lingering upon the man across the aisle as he stared at her creamy thigh. Jessie jerked the derringer free of the holster and swung it in an arc toward her lecherous neighbor. He nodded with embarrassment, then gulped at the sight of the derringer. Jessie answered with a slight smile as she pushed her skirt back down her thigh and over her knee until it dropped to her ankle. She palmed the derringer, then watched Straw Hat advance, his headgear beginning to fill with other people's belongings.

Greed brightened Straw Hat's eyes as he came within two rows of Jessie. He began to glance from the hat toward Jessie, winking his covetous eyes and baring his tobacco-stained teeth in a sneering grin. "Now, girlee, you should've sat in my lap when you got on the train. I would've let you keep your valuables."

Bowing her head to cast a furtive glance at Ki, Jessie saw the second robber approaching the *ninja*. Ki was like a coiled spring about to burst free. With so many people around, it would be dangerous to take on the two robbers, but Jessie knew it wasn't in Ki's constitution nor her own to let these ruffians have their way.

Straw Hat came to Jessie's row, shoving his hat past her face to the elderly couple beyond her. "Pay up, Mom and Pop," Straw Hat barked as his lecherous eyes stared at Jessie. "Be quick about it."

The elderly man freed his wallet, while his wife took off a modest necklace and dropped it atop the other valuables in his hat.

Straw Hat leaned toward Jessie. She hid the derringer, certain she couldn't miss at this range. Only problem was, Straw Hat now blocked her view of Ki down the aisle. If only they could act in concert and maintain the element of mutual surprise.

Then, Jessie heard the second robber growl. "Where's your money, Chink?"

"In my vest pocket," Ki answered.

Jessie knew that Ki carried more than money in his vest pockets. That was where he kept his *shuriken*.

"Then get your money," the robber commanded.

Jessie knew the moment of truth was approaching as Straw Hat waved his gun in her face. Jessie held her closed hand palm down over the hat.

Behind Straw Hat she heard his confused partner. "What the hell is that shiny thing? A damn Chink trinket?"

"Now, Jessie," Ki shouted.

Instantly the second robber screamed and stumbled backward.

Straw Hat twisted around. "What the hell?"

Jessie's fingers slid easily around the derringer as she aimed it. She saw the second robber recoil down the aisle, a throwing star embedded in his chest around a growing splotch of red.

49

Straw Hat dropped his booty and swung his six-shooter around toward Ki. "You damn Chink," he yelled.

Jessie leaped up and shoved the derringer against his ribs. "What?" he yelled.

Her fingers tightened around trigger and one barrel of the .38-caliber derringer popped, the discharge muffled by his shirt and flesh. Straw Hat stood in wide-eyed disbelief, staring at his shirt, which started to flame from the point-blank explosion of powder. His gun hand began to descend and his shoulders began to sag. He stumbled against the man who had stared at Jessie's thighs, then dropped his gun and slapped at the small patch of burning material. The flame disappeared beneath his now-bloody hand. His knees began to sag. Then he collapsed on the floor, his eyes rolling upward in his head.

Now Jessie could see Ki. He had jumped from his window position over two startled passengers and landed in the aisle. He grabbed the second robber's gun before he could fire it and wound some innocent victim. This robber's face was distorted with pain and surprise. He kept slapping at the razor-sharp throwing star in his chest, trying to knock away the pain but only succeeding in driving the star deeper in his chest and cutting his hands.

Jessie bent over Straw Hat and picked up his .45-caliber revolver from the floor. "There's more in the next passenger car, Ki," she called. "Robbing the passengers was the sideshow. The government payroll in the baggage car is the main attraction."

Ki nodded. "I just wish we knew how many."

"Didn't the conductor say four? We saw two of them come in here to talk with these two."

All around Jessie and Ki, the passengers who had sat silently stunned at what they saw began to shout and scream, some calling for their valuables, others panicking, afraid that more robbers would come in and kill them in retribution. A few men volunteered to help Jessie and Ki take on the others.

Quickly the noise grew so loud that Jessie feared the

robbers in the next passenger car would realize something was amiss. Jessie waved her arms over her head. "Hush," she called, "hush!"

She pointed to the man who had been staring at her thigh. "Drag this one to the back of the car and hide his body." The man hesitated. "Move it," she called, waving the derringer in his face. When he leaned down and grabbed Straw Hat, Jessie lifted her skirt and slid her derringer into the garter holster. She gave Straw Hat's revolver to a wide-eyed man and pulled her own pistol free.

Ki squeezed past her, dragging the second bandit to the back and shoving him under the feet of some passengers.

"Calm down, everyone, calm down," Jessie called as she moved to the front of the passenger car. "Your lives depend on it. Be quiet and lift your hands so if the others check this car they'll think everything is okay."

A few hesitated until Jessie waved her six-shooter over their heads. Instantly, everybody obliged and began to calm down. "How can we help?" a couple men called.

"Just sit and be quiet with your hands in the air. Ki, there's four at least in the next car."

Ki darted back down the aisle to Jessie and motioned for her to slide into the seats vacated by the bandits. That would make it harder for the thugs from the other car to see them if they glanced through the door window.

From the next car came the retort of a gun. Then a second, third, and fourth shot echoed through the passenger car. Jessie peeked from around the seat and through the door window into the next car. Despite the shots, what passengers she could see were sitting with their hands above their heads.

"Anybody hurt?" Ki asked as he leaned over behind her.

"I don't think so. The robbers may be shooting the lock off the express car door. They're after the government payroll. We've got to stop them, but we've only got one direction of attack."

Ki pulled Jessie from in front of the door. "No, we have two," Ki said, ripping off his coat and tossing it on the seat.

"Two?"

Nodding, Ki patted his vests counting the throwing stars available to him. "You from behind, me from above."

"What?"

Ki slid the sheath that carried his curve-bladed *tanto* from the side of his trousers to the front. "I'll leave by the back, crawl over the passenger cars, then drop into the express car, give them a little surprise."

"What do you want me to do?"

Falling onto the vacant seat, Ki pulled off his Wellington boots and dropped them on the floor. "Better grip and less noise on the roof," he explained. For a moment he considered Jessie's question. "Watch through the window. When I jump into things, see if you can pick the nearest one off." Ki shot up from his seat and darted back down the aisle.

"Good luck," Jessie said as he exited the passenger compartment.

Ki stepped onto the platform, quickly closing the door behind him. The night was brisk, and he shivered at the air rushing around the car and slapping against him. It would only get worse when he climbed on top. He caught his breath, then grabbed the metal rail that supported the canopy over the back platform and shimmied up onto the roof, collapsing on his stomach. The wind slammed into his face, screamed into his ears, and bloated his mouth until his cheeks bulged. Between the roar of the wind and the clickety-clack of the rails, he was deaf to everything else. The car rolled along with a swaying motion that had not been nearly so pronounced inside.

Slowly he pushed himself up to his hands and knees, then to his feet, and began to advance in a crouch. The wind punched him like a gigantic fist, and his face stung from the impact of minute cinders and smoke that blew back over the train. It was slow going as he inched forward into the howling wind, taking his time to be sure he could maintain his balance. From the express car he thought he heard the sound of another gunshot, but he could not be sure, not with the wind rushing by his ear.

The car was bathed in a dull moonlight that gave everything a deathly gray pallor, but helped Ki advance with more confidence than if the night had been moonless. The locomotive chugged and puffed, then hit a wide curve. The momentum threatened to throw Ki from his elevated perch, but he fell flat on the roof, his fingernails digging into the very paint of the wood. He cursed in Japanese, but his words were lost even to himself in the onrushing wind. Every time he looked forward, his eyes became targets for streaking cinders. Screening his eyes with one hand, he used the other to push himself back up into a crouch and continue toward the express car.

This was taking longer than he had anticipated, and he hoped Jessie had not grown impatient. The car that looked so short inside the passenger compartment now from the roof seemed so much longer than fifty feet.

Ki advanced to the midway point of the car, then stomped on the roof with his foot to let Jessie know he was okay and still advancing.

Walking became more and more difficult as the wind tried to rip his clothes from his body. Ki cursed again to the wind, then fell to his belly and began to snake forward, keeping his eyes closed as much as he could. Finally, he reached the end of the car and knew he was right above Jessie. He knocked on the wood to signal his location. Though he could not hear her answering knock, he thought he felt its vibration on the roof.

Squinting his eyes against the prickle of the flying cinders and the blast of the wind, Ki gauged the distance between the two cars. Without the wind, a child could make the jump, but against the howling gusts any man would have difficulty, particularly since he couldn't get a running start at it, and especially since Ki had to land lightly to keep from arousing suspicions of the robbers inside.

Ki eased as near the edge of the roof as he dared, then

crouched into a ball, his leg muscles like coiled springs about to explode. He caught his breath and shoved himself away from the edge of one roof for the next. He sprang ahead like a panther leaping for prey and landed roughly on the next roof, harder than he had anticipated. He hoped he hadn't made too much noise. He relaxed flat against the roof and put his ear against the wood, hoping he could hear something inside that would indicate if he had raised the alarm. He heard nothing but the deafening wind.

Slowly, he began to snake forward. He had to be careful now not to make any noises that would give him away. Ki had lost track of time, but time didn't matter now as much as success. He inched forward, considering his options once he reached the gap between the passenger car and the express car. He suspected he could take out at least one robber, possibly with a throwing star, as he passed between the two cars, but that would likely raise the alarm and leave him to deal with three others. However, against such a strong head wind, he didn't know how accurate the *shuriken* would be.

Or he might swing down between the cars and attack those in the express car, hoping the element of surprise would allow him to debilitate them before they had a chance to react. Even so, that would still leave at least one, maybe two of the robbers at his back in the passenger car. Jessie was a good shot, but she might not know to fire until she heard shots, and by then it might be too late.

Ki reached the halfway point on the passenger car, and paused to let his breath catch up with his physical effort. His eyes were dry and painful from the soot and occasional cinder flakes.

He held his hand to his mouth and spit in it, then rubbed at his eyes to try to massage some moisture back into them. He had had enough time atop the train, and decided to swing down between the two cars and take his chances with those in the express car. He just hoped Jessie was able to cover his back. He lay with his eyes shut for a minute or more, knowing he had to work out the dryness to keep it from

54

interfering with his sight when he finally decided to attack.

The moon went behind a cloud and the night grew dimmer. Ki gritted his teeth, then started to inch forward on his belly again, occasionally looking ahead.

That was when he saw a shadowy figure climb over the far end of the express car. He was crouched low to keep the rushing wind from knocking him off. In his hand, he carried a revolver.

Ki blinked his eyes, trying to moisten them, but the onrushing wind dried them out so quickly that Ki had to squint to see, and even then he could barely make out more than the form of a man.

And still the man advanced!

Ki squeezed his eyelids tight for a minute as he slipped his hand into a vest pocket and tugged out a *shuriken*. The wind whistled around his shoulder and tried to jerk the throwing star from between his fingers.

When Ki opened his eyes and began to ease up on his hands and knees, the approaching figure was obscured by the plume of locomotive smoke carried by the wind over the railroad cars. The soot stung Ki's eyes and face.

For a brief moment the shadowy figure emerged from the smoke, seeming more intent on keeping his footing than on spotting Ki. Ki did not understand why the man who had apparently been sent on the roof after him was so careless. Blind luck was all Ki could figure.

Ki had never thrown a *shuriken* from such an awkward position, and never against such a fierce wind. Still on his hands and knees, he twisted around sideways and drew his right arm under his chest. The wind was tearing at his eyes when the figure emerged from the haze.

It was then or never! With all the strength he could muster, Ki threw his arm, then flicked his wrist.

That was the moment Ki recognized the Texas Ranger Wade Shaw.

"Shaw," he screamed at the top of his lungs.

Instantly, the Ranger toppled to the roof.

★

Chapter 7

Ki caught his breath. The *shuriken* had left his hand before he recognized Shaw. Ki saw the star but for a moment, then it disappeared in the darkness. Shaw fell to the rooftop and the wind—or maybe worse, the *shuriken*—knocked the Ranger's hat off and it flew by.

"What was that?" came a voice from the express car.

"There's somebody on the roof," answered another.

Ki eased away from the edge of the passenger car, his glance alternating between the fallen Ranger and the door to the express car. His hand fell to his vest for another throwing star. When he glanced back toward the locomotive, he saw Shaw stirring, wiping the side of his head.

The Ranger looked up, realized Ki was atop the next car, and waved his hand to let him know he was okay.

Ki let out a long breath, but he didn't have time to consider Shaw's close call.

A gunshot rang out from the express car and a hole splintered in the roof not two feet from Shaw. Yellow lamplight from inside the car leaked through the hole out of the express car. Then came another shot and another.

"Keep him busy while I climb up and shoot him off," called an excited voice from inside.

Shaw scooted along the roof, trying to outguess the unseen outlaws below.

Ki backed farther from the edge of the passenger car so he could not be seen from the door of the express car. He heard a commotion below, and then saw a man's head and shoulders appear as he climbed up the express car and propped his arm and gun over the roof.

His eyes squinting against the wind, Ki pulled his arm under his chest and flung a throwing star at the gunman. The *shuriken* landed solidly between the man's spine and the shoulder of his gun hand. As the sharp metal embedded itself in the man's flesh, the bandit loosed a high-pitched scream and his revolver slid from his hand and over the edge of the express car. By instinct the bandit reached for the gun and lost his grip, falling from his perch to the platform below, then tumbling over the side of the train, his scream ending in a muffled thump that was lost in the clickety-clack of the iron wheels over iron rails.

One down, three to go, Ki thought as he glanced down the length of the express car and saw Shaw coming toward him, still dodging gunshots through the roof. Just then, Ki heard a gunshot explode in the passenger care below him. He heard a scream.

"Damnation, woman, where'd you come from?" shouted another voice.

With Jessie showing her hand, it was time to get involved before she got hurt. Ki freed another *shuriken* from his vest and crawled to the edge of the passenger car, then jumped for the platform on the express car. He landed nimbly, then bolted past the broken door into the car's bright yellow light. For an instant, he was blinded.

"Who the hell are you?" he heard a man scream.

Quickly his eyes adjusted to the lamplight, and he saw two bandits scrambling to reload their revolvers. Ki flung his throwing star at the farthest one, who instantly screamed and grabbed his now-empty gun arm. That one would be immobilized for a moment.

Ki lunged toward the other bandit and in one fluid motion pulled the *tanto* from his waistband. The bandit's eyes went wide with terror as the knife arched for his chest. By reflex, the man threw up his gun hand and deflected the knife with the barrel of his gun. Ki jumped back from the bandit, a big man with a crooked nose and crumpled ears, then darted toward him as he fumbled with his free hand to pull a bullet from his cartridge belt.

Behind him, Ki heard another gunshot, then another in the passenger car. He hoped Jessie could hold on long enough for him to finish off this one and provide her with reinforcements.

Ki feinted with the knife for the big man's abundant gut, and when his hand dropped to protect his belly, Ki sliced across the top of it with the knife. The gun fell with a clatter to the floor and the terrified bandit held up his bloody hand and stared at his dangling thumb. His eyes rolled up to the top of his eyelids and he fainted dead away. Just then, Ki saw a movement from beside a pile of mail sacks and prepared to throw his knife in that direction, until he recognized the uniform of an express car clerk.

"Get their guns," Ki ordered as he spun around and ran back toward the passenger car.

Wade Shaw, the side of his face streaked with blood, slid from the express car onto the platform just as Ki rushed by.

Ki jumped into the passenger car, holding his knife to throw it if necessary. He was relieved to see Jessie standing over another bandit lying in the aisle and using his finger to plug the gunshot wound in his bloody shoulder.

Jessie offered Ki a perplexed nod, then shook the business end of her revolver. "I'm a better shot than he is. Are you okay, Ki? I heard a lot of shooting and you don't look too good."

"Not a scratch," Ki replied, puzzled by her remark.

"Wipe your face," she instructed.

Ki shrugged and lifted his sleeve to his cheek. It was then

58

he realized his shirt had turned gray from the soot it had caught on the roof. He pulled the sleeve across his cheek and lips, then stared at an even bigger and darker smudge of soot from his face. He caught a glimpse of himself in the reflection of the nearest window and realized his face was filthy.

He was about to answer Jessie when he heard Shaw stride in behind him.

"Wade," called Jessie, "you're hurt?"

Ki saw the concern in Jessie's eyes as she stepped around the bandit and hurried to Shaw.

"It's not as bad as it looks," Shaw offered, his drawn gun pointed at the bandit on the floor, "though a damn close shave your boy, Ki, gave me."

"What?" Jessie said, spinning around to stare at Ki.

"Ki, what happened?" she demanded.

Before Ki could speak, Shaw came to his defense. "I didn't realize he was on the roof when I made it atop the express car. He must've figured I was one of them."

Jessie brushed her hand softly against his bloodied cheek, then touched his ear. "He sliced off the bottom of your earlobe."

"One of them damn throwing stars," Shaw replied. "If he hadn't have yelled, I'd taken it full in the face, I guess."

Ki stepped toward the Ranger. "Once he yelled, the robbers started shooting through the roof. Just one thing, Shaw. Why didn't you look down the roof? Surely you'd have spotted me."

Shaw offered an embarrassed grin. "I didn't figure on there being another fool up there, and . . ." Shaw let his sentence die in the air.

"And what?" Ki asked.

Shaw grimaced, "And I'm afraid of heights."

Ki grinned.

"Way I figure it, Ki," Shaw offered, "I'd rather face a dozen of your throwing stars than another minute atop that damn express car. Now, we better herd all these fellows together in the baggage car so we can see what we've got. Something still bothers me about this robbery."

"There's two more in the back car," Jessie said.

"There's two in the express car and this one," Shaw said, his gun pointed at the man's head.

"One fell off the train and is likely dead back down the tracks," Ki added.

"That totals six," Shaw said, scanning the passenger car and the hushed crowd, then motioning for the conductor to come forward.

Still trembling, the conductor stood up from his aisle seat.

"Do you know how many there were?" Shaw asked him.

"Six, best I could tell."

Shaw nodded and commanded the conductor to get some men to drag the two from the back. "Are they dead?" Shaw asked Jessie.

"Don't know for sure," Jessie replied. "Just that they weren't feeling well when we left."

Shaw laughed and motioned with his gun for the bandit on the floor to rise and march into the express car.

Gritting his teeth at the pain, the bandit managed to make it to his feet and stumble into the express car ahead of Shaw, Jessie, and Ki. The wounded robber fell onto the mail sacks beside his two wounded compatriots.

A second uniformed express clerk had materialized from somewhere and stood alongside the one Ki remembered. Both covered the bandits with their own revolvers.

Shortly, men from the back passenger car dragged the other two bandits inside. Straw Hat was dead and his companion wounded and groaning.

Shaw pointed to the mail sacks. "Drag them over there." He turned to the conductor. "Any passengers hurt?"

"No, sir," the conductor's voice quivered. "Nothing except everybody's a little jittery right now."

Jessie nodded. "Nothing to worry about."

Shaw shook his head. "One thing doesn't add up."

"What?" Jessie asked.

"Once they got the money, what were they going to do? How were they going to escape?" the Ranger replied.

Precisely, thought Ki. They had to have an ally somewhere waiting for them. Once they had taken all the money, they would've stopped the train where a confederate would be waiting with horses.

Ki and Shaw strode to the wounded gang members.

"Where were you gonna stop the train?" Shaw demanded.

"How many men with the horses?" Ki piped in.

The robbers just stared defiantly ahead.

"Damn you all, talk," Shaw demanded. Receiving no answer, the Ranger strode over to the one still plugging his shoulder wound with his finger. Shaw bent down and jerked it out of the bullet hole.

The robber screamed and tried to shake his arm from Shaw's iron grip. "Let go."

"Tell me," Shaw insisted, "or I'll stand here and hold your hand until you bleed to death."

The robber looked from the Ranger to his confederates, then turned away from their hate-filled glares.

Shaw squeezed the man's hand harder. "Tell me."

The wounded man gulped, then spoke at a whisper so low that nobody could hear him except the adjacent robber, who kicked him with his boot.

Ki walked beside the man with the errant boot. It was the big man who had fainted after Ki had nearly sliced off his thumb. "Leave your friend alone," Ki ordered, "before I cut your thumb completely off." The big man's pale face grew even whiter.

"Now," said Shaw to the first robber, "where were you to stop for the rest of your gang? And speak so I can hear you and won't have to ask again."

"Bent Creek crossing," he replied.

Shaw looked to the express car clerks. "How far until Bent Creek?"

One of the clerks pulled his pocket watch and checked the

time. "About ten minutes," he replied, snapping the watch shut.

The Ranger turned back to the robber and released his hand. "How many many will be waiting?"

The robber plugged his shoulder with his finger. "Just one."

Shaw nodded. "Jessie, you help the clerks here keep an eye on these fellows while Ki and I let the engineer know we need to stop and pick up one more passenger."

Ki pointed at the pockmarked roof. "Want to climb back over the top?"

Shaw shook his head and pointed at the door at the front end of the express car. "We'll unlock that and crawl over the tender. I've spent all the time I ever want to spend atop a moving railroad car."

One of the express clerks scurried to the front, unlocked a padlock, and opened the door. Shaw led Ki out the door, then climbed atop the tender car and worked his way over the pile of coal. The fireman clanged shut the furnace door and watched Shaw and Ki step into the cover of the cab.

"Everybody okay?" asked the fireman.

"All except the robbers," Shaw answered.

The engineer, preoccupied with watching the track in the glow of the locomotive's bright lamp, glanced briefly over his shoulder, then stared back out of the metal monster plunging ahead.

Pointing at Ki, the fireman spoke. "Who's he?"

"My deputy," Shaw said. "How far are we from Bent Creek?"

"Five or six minutes," the engineer replied. "How come?"

"Another gang member is waiting there with their horses. We need to stop and arrest him."

The engineer lifted the cap from his head, then pulled it snugly back in place. "It'll throw us off schedule."

Shaw grasped the engineer's shoulder firmly. "We'll stop," he announced. "A few minutes' delay in your schedule can save us days of tracking this last bandit."

"You're the law," the engineer replied. He relaxed the throttle valve lever and the locomotive began to slow, imperceptibly at first, then more noticeably. The engineer stuck his head out the cab. "Two, maybe three minutes to Bent Creek."

Shaw motioned for the fireman to move closer to the boiler. "Stay out of sight in case there's shooting." He looked at Ki. "You too."

Ki shrugged, refusing to acknowledge an order he might have to ignore.

"About a minute," the engineer said, "just around this bend."

The train began to curve to the right and then straighten as it headed for a small iron bridge.

"There's the bridge," the engineer called.

Shaw slipped up behind him. "And there's our man on the other side of the bridge." Shaw pulled his pistol from his holster. "Stop short of him so I can see him in the light."

That wasn't wise, Ki thought as he caught a glimpse of the bandit with the extra horses. Far better for the locomotive to pull past the outlaw to block him from crossing the tracks and escaping into the trees than to keep him in the beam of the bright lamp.

The locomotive slowed to a crawl as it reached the bridge. Then the engineer pulled on the brake lever. The locomotive inched to a stop just short of the end of the bridge, then loosed a final long hiss of steam that was replaced by slow rhythmic gasps.

"How'd it go?" the robber called.

"We're rich," Shaw answered from behind the engineer.

"Yeehaw," the robber whooped.

Crouching, Ki slipped away from the boiler and eased to the back of the cab, then down the steps to the rail bed, his socked feet crunching against the gravel. He slipped his hand into a vest pocket and retrieved a *shuriken,* just in case.

Shaw called. "Bring the horses in closer, we got us a wounded one."

Ki slipped to the front of the locomotive and squatted behind the cowcatcher. He watched the rider across the tracks begin to lead the other horses toward Shaw.

"Who's hurt?" the bandit called.

"Huh," Shaw said, trying to delay as long as possible the bandit's realization that he was talking with an impostor.

"Who's hurt?" the bandit repeated, then stopped, straightened, and stood in his stirrups. With his hands, he screened his eyes from the bright glare of the lamp. "Who are you?" he finally asked.

"Texas Ranger Wade Shaw," he said, stepping out of the cab, his gun drawn and pointed at the robber. "You're under arrest."

"Damnation," the robber said, settling back down in the saddle.

"Throw down your pistol," Shaw commanded.

The bandit's hand slowly went to his side, then flashed for the weapon, jerking it cleanly from his holster as he spurred the flank of his mount. He squeezed off a shot, which clanged off the locomotive's tempered metal.

Shaw fired, but the horse had already turned and was aiming to cross the railroad tracks.

Ki jumped up and cocked his arm, then flung the throwing star at the escaping rider. Ki watched the sudden flight of the *shuriken* in the glare of the lamp.

The rider screamed when the razor-sharp star sank into his chest, then collapsed from his mount. Ki darted to the downed man before he could react and wrenched the pistol from his hand. He stood covering the final gang member with his own pistol by the time Shaw rounded the end of the locomotive.

Shaw ran up behind Ki, who couldn't help but offer a smirk.

"I throw my stars better than you wear yours," Ki said.

Shaw patted at his own earlobe, earlier bloodied by an errant toss of Ki's *shuriken,* and responded with a sardonic smile.

★

Chapter 8

From the train trestle that connected the mainland with the island, Jessie could see Galveston before her. The city itself was clumped on the eastern end of the island where the docks and vast warehouses, several of them belonging to the Starbuck empire, were clustered. Most of the cotton grown in Texas passed through Galveston on its way to textile mills in the Northeast and to the few that were beginning to locate elsewhere on the East Coast. On the distant docks Jessie could see bales of cotton standing in close ranks like bloated dominoes.

Because of its long domination of the seacoast trade, Galveston was the financial center of Texas, though it was finding itself more and more in competition with other cities trying to take away that title. The Strand was Galveston's financial district and as attractive a street as any to be found in Texas. The street showed its wealth with fine brick structures of Gothic Revival, Italianate, and Second Empire architecture. The Strand was just a couple of blocks from docks that jutted out into Galveston Bay. The island itself screened the bay from the Gulf of Mexico and provided good harbor for the dozens of steamships and sailing vessels that made Galveston calls to pick up freight or passengers.

Galveston Island was a sand barrier island that looked like a giant splinter from the mainland. The island stretched some twenty-seven miles in length, but barely reached three miles in width at its widest point. It had once been the home of the pirate Jean Lafitte, and the island's sandy soils were pitted with the holes of Sunday afternoon treasure hunters who still dug for the buried gold Lafitte was rumored to have left behind.

As the train neared the island, Jessie could see the mud flats and salt marshes that rimmed the bay. Herons and ducks had taken up positions in the shallows as they dined on the bay's rich bounty. Beyond the island, Jessie could see the Gulf's deep blue waters, which broke in white-crowned waves upon the distant beaches.

She was glad to be nearing her destination, though she was uncertain whether Shaw's plan to spirit her away somewhere in secrecy was still working. After all, word would get out of the attempted train robbery and the part a striking young woman and her Eurasian companion had had in stopping the crime. Only Jessie and Ki, the Lone Star Legend as some newspapers had taken to calling them, matched that description. Still, Jessie had not responded to Lord Clinton Bly's proposal by telegraph or letter, so no one in Galveston knew of her impending arrival. The secrecy of the trip was not helped by the death of two of the seven robbers. Wade Shaw had gotten off the train at the next town to jail the outlaws and attend to the required Ranger and legal details that accompanied death, even of outlaws. Once he completed the paperwork, he would resume his journey to Galveston. He'd promised to join her as soon as he could, and Jessie relished his arrival.

Jessie did not know how to assess Ki's relationship with the Texas Ranger. She thought a grudging respect had been established between the two, but she still suspected some jealousy on Ki's part. Out of the corner of her eye, she glanced at Ki, and couldn't help but snicker at the smudges of soot that still ringed his face. The facilities on this passenger car were not nearly so commodious as those on her Pullman, and Ki had been unable to do more than smear it worse. Ki stared sullenly ahead, though she attributed his mood to exhaustion and the embarrassment of looking like a slovenly worker.

As the train began the gentle descent down the trestle toward the island, Ki stretched in his seat and began to study the ships on the bay. When the train pulled into the modest station, Jessie and Ki stood and followed the many passengers out of the car and onto the platform. The air was heavy with moisture and the salty aroma of the bay not three blocks distant. A couple of passengers who had ridden all the way from the capital thanked them a final time for thwarting the robbery and saving their valuables and their lives.

Jessie responded graciously for herself and for Ki, then moved through the station with Ki in her wake. She drew the admiring glances of several men, but paid attention to only one—a short, compact man with muscled and tattooed arms that hung from the ragged sleeves of a sailor's blouse. Through the plume of smoke from his ivory pipe, he stared at her with a single eye, his left being covered by a black patch. His ruddy face was partially obscured by a ragged beard that seemed to hide a crooked scar down his left cheek.

Ki spotted him too. "A common thief, the man with the eye patch," he said.

"But why is he staring at us, Ki? I'm dirty and you're filthy. We're carrying no luggage. What could he see in us?"

"Maybe it's The Scorpion." There was a note of derision in Ki's voice.

They exited the train station side by side and walked down the street, passing the city hall and marshal's office on their way to the Crown Hotel, their customary residence during Galveston visits. Jessie glanced back over her shoulder and caught a glimpse of the suspicious man trailing them. "He's following us, Ki."

"I know," Ki answered, taking Jessie's arm and steering her through the strolling pedestrians.

As they crossed a side street, Jessie looked toward the docks and was surprised to see a huge white paddle wheel steamer, its paint gleaming and its deck immaculate, flying the Union Jack. The ship's tall white smokestack was adorned with a golden "B" embedded in a black diamond. "That must be Lord Clinton Bly's yacht," she said.

Ki slowed down, looking around for the man with the eye patch. "We lost him, but it doesn't make sense, losing him so easily."

"Maybe we're imagining too much, Ki."

The *ninja* shrugged.

Jessie stopped on the corner and stared at the massive yacht. "A gaudy display of wealth," she mused. "I doubt we could have any conceivable mutual interests."

Ki stamped his foot impatiently as he studied the passing pedestrians. "Let's just get to the hotel and get cleaned up."

Jessie heard impatience in his voice, and turned her gaze from the dock to Ki. She thought she saw concern in his eyes, but maybe it was just the embarrassment of being so dirty in public. She nodded. "We could both use a bath and new clothes for our stay," she said as she plunged ahead.

The Crown stood at the end of the block. A three-story brick building with a drive that passed beneath a carriage portico shading the entrance, the Crown and its stable covered the entire block. Jessie always stayed in the Crown's Grand Suite, which opened atop the carriage portico. The roof of the portico doubled as the suite's balcony.

Ki and Jessie moved quickly down the street, and were soon climbing the front steps of the Crown. A couple of dowagers with wide hips and slender noses sniffed at the dirty clothes of Jessie and Ki as he opened the Crown's ornate door. Ki allowed Jessie to pass, all the time scowling at the two arrogant old ladies. They seemed reluctant to exit. When they finally decided to accept an act of courtesy from someone so far beneath their station in life, they took a confident step forward, only to have Ki release the door and slide past them inside.

Jessie held a chuckle. "That was uncalled for."

"So was their attitude."

Jessie and Ki walked across the broad lobby, its walls covered with Oriental tapestries and its floors strewn with thick carpets, plush sofas, and chairs. Jessie and Ki approached the desk, and drew a disapproving glare, then a look of amazement from the clerk when they stopped before him.

"Miss Starbuck?" he asked, his eyes wide with disbelief.

Jessie held her fingers up to her lips. "Shhh," she said, "we're on a surprise visit here."

He nodded very gravely. "So that's why you're traveling like the lower class," he said, taking in their soiled clothes and their need for a bath.

"I would like the Grand Suite, and the adjacent suite for Ki."

The clerk's expression turned as stiff as his starched collar. "I'm afraid it's taken." He leaned over the counter toward Jessie, looked up and down the lobby, then spoke in a conspiratorial whisper. "Lord Clinton Bly, the English industrialist, has taken it. Had we known you were coming, we would have reserved it for you."

Jessie nodded. "We'll take the best you've got left. We're tired and in quick need of a bath in case you hadn't noticed."

The clerk nodded. "Yes, ma'am, I mean, no, ma'am, I hadn't noticed. Any luggage?"

From Jessie's skewered glance at her clothes and then her laugh, the clerk realized it was a foolish question.

"Have one of your dress shops send over a couple changes of clothes for me, and see that a tailor provides clothes for Ki. We'll need traveling outfits like we're now wearing, as well as clothes for business and clothes for entertainment."

"Yes, ma'am," the clerk said, and rang a desk bell for a bellboy to show Jessie and Ki to their suites.

They followed the black bellboy up the stairs to their rooms. As the bellboy opened the door to Jessie's room, she glanced at Ki. "Let's take a good long bath and give the new clothes time to arrive. Then let's meet, say in two hours, and

69

make a trip to the Starbuck Cotton Exporters and see what Martin Bark knows about Lord Clinton Bly's visit."

With Jessie at his side, Ki marched down the stairs to the lobby of the Crown Hotel. Both showed the results of long baths and new clothes. They now were presentable, though Ki was not entirely comfortable. Too, he had had to have his vest cleaned, and he would emerge onto the streets of Galveston without his full arsenal of throwing stars. He had put a couple in his suit pocket, just in case, but he still felt naked without the vest. As the pair marched past the registration desk, the wiry clerk stopped sorting mail and motioned to Jessie.

Ki followed her to the desk, where the clerk leaned toward her and looked both ways down the lobby before whispering to her. "Miss Starbuck," he said, "we will move your things to the Grand Suite while you are out."

Jessie shook her head. "I don't understand."

"Lord Clinton Bly heard of your arrival and learned he was staying in your accustomed room."

Ki stepped up to the desk beside Jessie. "Who told him of our arrival?"

The clerk gulped. "Not me. I mean, he sent his assistant to the desk asking questions as if he knew you were here. I merely mentioned that Lord Bly was staying in your suite. His assistant came back shortly, saying Lord Bly was prepared to give up the Grand Suite for your use."

Ki thought the clerk was lying. More likely the clerk had asked Lord Bly to vacate the room, hoping to draw a big tip from Jessie, who was a more frequent visitor to Galveston than Lord Bly. Ki didn't like it, word of their Galveston arrival being so easily bandied about.

Jessie asked the clerk, "Did Lord Bly give a reason for his departure?"

Now rattled with worry that he might be in trouble over his part in securing the Grand Suite for Jessie, the clerk licked his lips. "His assistant merely said that he had business interests to discuss with you and did not care to alienate you before discussing those matters."

From Jessie's nod, Ki knew she thought the explanation was plausible, but he was still uncertain. He didn't like this coincidence. Jessie slipped her hand in her pocket, pulling out her key and sliding it on the desk to the clerk. "Ki," she started, but before she could go on, he dropped his key beside hers.

"Will there be anything else, Miss Starbuck?" the clerk asked.

"No, thank you," she said, turning and heading for the door.

Ki lingered a moment, staring at the clerk. "You didn't tell them of our arrival?"

"No, sir," the clerk promised.

Ki spun around and quickly caught up with Jessie. He didn't know whether or not to believe the clerk.

Emerging from the Crown Hotel, Jessie headed down the busy street to the corner, turning on the side street that paralleled the side of the hotel and led to the docks. Ki could feel her glance. "You're too suspicious, Ki."

"How did Lord Bly know of our arrival so quickly? We sent no telegram, no message of any kind that we were arriving."

"It's coincidence, nothing more, Ki."

"Odd coincidence?"

"Not as odd a coincidence as the two robbery attempts against us trying to leave the capital. The two that stopped us in the buggy didn't know who we were, nor did the gang on the train. It's just coincidence."

Ki nodded his head, but he didn't agree. Something seemed odd to his sense of cosmic order. If he was a suspicious man, it was suspicion based upon deviations from the natural permutations of nature and man.

Near the end of the block, they passed the alleyway that led to the Crown Hotel Stable, which provided fine mounts and carriages for guests. The stable building was separated

71

from the hotel itself by the alleyway that led off the side street where they walked, then turned at a ninety-degree angle and exited onto the back street. The building was a luxurious stable, one that might have been mistaken for a small office building were it not for the faint aroma of horseflesh and droppings.

"Perhaps we shall have time for some riding," Jessie said.

Again Ki nodded, but without enthusiasm. He could ride. In fact his Oriental horsemanship far exceeded the skills of the average cowboy on the Circle Star, and rivaled the horseback expertise of the fabled Comanches. Even so, he much preferred to be unburdened by a horse, especially during what leisure he allowed himself in his continuing efforts to protect Jessie.

Past the stable, they turned down the back street and made their way two blocks to the office of Starbuck Cotton Exporters. It was a narrow, three-story building that sat innocuously between a pair of broad two-story offices that dominated the rest of the block. Though the other two offices, one a shipping insurance firm and the second an importer, had bold signs proclaiming their names, the Starbuck office had discreet lettering on the window and nothing more. But the Starbuck office controlled a dozen warehouses and half that many docks along the bay, not to mention the cotton compress and assorted ancillary enterprises.

As Ki pushed open the door, a bell at the top tinkled to announce their arrival, and a young red-haired man at the front desk looked up from a stack of manifests and greeted them with a smile. Behind him a dozen men and women worked at desks and at file cabinets, dealing with all sorts of information.

"May I help you?" the red-haired young man asked, taking in Ki and Jessie. His brow furrowed as if he should be making a connection that he wasn't.

"We're here to see Martin Bark," Jessie announced.

"He's awfully busy right now, ma'am, but I shall be glad to tell him you are here. Your name?"

Jessie smiled. "Jessica Starbuck."

The young man's smile collapsed into a sudden frown. "Yes, ma'am, Miss Starbuck," he said, jumping up from his swivel chair and looking at Ki. "You must be Ki, correct?"

Ki nodded.

"But yes, Mr. Bark has time to see you, Miss Starbuck, of course." He turned around and darted up the stairs, his footsteps echoing throughout the building. When he reached Martin Bark's office on the third floor, he announced Jessie's presence with such loud excitement that everyone downstairs could hear. They all turned and cast furtive glances at Jessie and Ki before resuming their work at an accelerated pace.

Instantly, the pounding footsteps began their descent back to the front. The red-haired man was scarcely down the stairs and at his desk before he panted an announcement. "Mr. Bark will see you shortly."

No sooner had the young man seated himself and tried to collect his breath than Martin Bark appeared from up the stairs. He was a gray-headed man with a matching close-cropped beard. Though he was nearing retirement, the years had treated him as well as he had treated the Starbuck business. He was lean and vibrant and dressed in a freshly pressed suit. He would pass for a man twenty years younger were it not for the reading glasses hanging from a chain around his neck.

He held out his hand as he approached his visitors. "Jessie," he said, "you're as beautiful as ever, looking more and more like your mother every day."

Ki could see the pleasure in Jessie's eyes at the remark.

"And Ki, it is an honor to see you again."

"Thank you, sir."

Bark gestured with his arm toward the stairs. "Would you care to join me in my office?"

"Certainly, Marty," Jessie replied. "You are as charming as ever."

Bark smiled, but Ki thought he detected a glimmer of concern in his eyes.

73

"How's business?" Jessie asked.

"Fine," Bark said without enthusiasm as they topped the second flight of stairs and headed for his office.

"Climbing these stairs everyday must be what's kept you in such fit form," Jessie offered.

Bark opened his office door and allowed Jessie and Ki to pass. He entered behind them and closed the door.

Jessie and Ki moved to the leather chairs opposite his broad desk. Behind his desk, a wide window offered a view of the bay and all its activity.

He eased to his desk and collapsed in his chair. "I was worried when I didn't receive an answer to my telegram."

"We've been away from the Circle Star a few days, Marty," Jessie said. "What is it?"

Bark pursed his lips and shook his head. "We've got trouble, Jessie. Lord Clinton Bly."

★

Chapter 9

Jessie leaned forward in her chair. Marty was a manager she could trust implicitly. When he said there was trouble, Jessie was certain he was not exaggerating. "Tell me about it."

Bark let out a long sigh. "Just a few more years to retirement and now this."

Jessica laughed. "Marty, I'm not sure you'll ever retire and I'll be just as happy if you don't, as good an operation as you run."

"Thank you, Jessie, I appreciate your kind words. I guess I owe it to your father, a fine man who gave me a chance early on when I needed one. You've got your mother's looks, Jessie, but your father's business sense and rock-solid integrity."

With a nod, Jessie smiled. "Now go on about Lord Bly."

Bark stroked his gray beard. "Lord Bly arrived in town four days ago from New Orleans, so I am told. He's making all the Southern port cities, talking to all the cotton exporters." Bark paused. "Maybe threatening is a better word. Anyway, he's trying to persuade them all to unite with him and control the buying and selling of cotton worldwide."

"An ambitious man, isn't he?" Jessie offered.

"A dangerous one," Bark replied. "By controlling the

purchase price, he'll bring the cotton economy in Texas and the rest of the South to its knees. By controlling the selling price to textile mills worldwide, he'll become richer for sure, more powerful as an industrialist, and likely more dangerous."

Jessie nodded. "Starbuck Cotton Exporters just won't get involved with Lord Clinton Bly."

Bark nodded. "I knew that would be your answer, and likely Bly did too, because word going around the waterfront is that he's here to close a deal with us or take us over against our will. You and I know, Jessie, that he is one of the few men in the world with the power and resources to take on you and the Starbuck empire."

Jessie stood up from her chair and walked around Bark's desk to the wide window. She stood with her arms crossed, taking in the late afternoon activity at the docks and wharves. Her gaze, though, kept coming to rest on the gleaming white yacht emblazoned with the black diamond "B" on its smokestack. "I had heard of Lord Clinton Bly of course, Marty, and had received a telegram to come here to discuss items of mutual interest, but I had no idea he was such a dangerous man."

Bark eased out of his chair. "His ambitions extend beyond being just an English or European industrialist. He's now moving up to a world scale and has lost any scruples he ever had, and that's giving him credit for having had some." Bark paused. "We may be in for a battle, Jessie."

Jessie reached over and patted Martin Bark on the shoulder. "We'll do just fine."

Nodding slightly, Bark let out another long sigh. "I hope so. He's a shrewd one, though. I understand he's going from here to Mexico to take over the ports there. Apparently, he thinks once he gets control of all the cotton prices in the States, some farmers may try to move their cotton into Mexico, then sell it there for a price he can't control. To keep that from happening, he's said to be trying to take over the ports there so he can control them as well. That shows you how shrewd he is."

"Marty, don't you worry. Bly and I will have no business to discuss, thanks to your usual good job in providing me information. I trust your judgment, and will do everything within my power and within the resources of the Starbuck empire to keep our good name at arm's distance from Lord Clinton Bly."

A thin smile creased Bark's face for the first time since he had entered his office with Jessie and Ki. He invited Ki to the window, and began to refresh Jessie's memory by pointing out which docks, wharves, and warehouses belonged to the Starbuck empire. He pointed out five ships either tied up by the docks or anchored in the bay that were Starbuck vessels. He talked with the pride of a man who had managed his job and his resources well.

"Do you care to look at the books, Jessie?"

"It's not necessary, Marty."

"I understand, Jessie, and I know that is a vote of faith in me and my management. Nonetheless, I feel obligated to insist that you inspect the profit statement to make sure it pleases you."

"If you insist."

Bark pointed to his desk chair. "Please be seated and I shall return in just a moment."

He left the room, closing the door behind him.

"A good man," Jessie said to Ki.

"He is what Lord Clinton Bly seems not to be."

"We won't have to stay long in Galveston then, unless Marty needs our support. I'm anxious to get back to the ranch and help some more with the branding."

Ki said nothing, but from his expression Jessie knew he wasn't looking forward to any more ranch work. Jessie decided to tease Ki just a bit. "Of course, we can't leave Galveston until Wade Shaw catches up with us."

His eyes narrowing for just a moment, Ki seemed not as

antagonistic about the Ranger as he had been before. He shrugged.

"After all, we did promise the governor," she said.

Ki shrugged again. "You promised the governor, not me."

Jessie laughed. "We're a team, Ki, remember?" With her comment, she thought she drew a sliver of a grin from Ki as Bark entered the room, carrying a thick ledger that he plopped down on his desk.

"Take all the time you like, Jessie, and I'll be glad to answer questions about anything you might think irregular."

Jessie thanked him and began to look at the figures entered in the ledger. She knew they were in fine order, but she also knew that Bark expected her to inspect them rigidly. She spent about thirty minutes poring over the columns of numbers, occasionally asking a question.

Ki, with his habitual patience, stood at the window behind her, watching the changing activity at the port.

Closing the ledger, Jessie nodded at Bark. "Fine job, Marty. You've looked after our interests well."

"Thank you, Jessie, but that's what you pay me to do. Now, I should be delighted to take you and Ki to dinner this evening."

"We appreciate the invitation, Marty, but we've had a tiring trip just getting here and I think we'll dine at the hotel and retire early."

"Very well," he said as Jessie stood up.

Ki joined her and they followed Bark to the door.

"Allow me," said Bark, "to introduce you to some of our new employees."

Though Jessie had reservations about the knowledge of her presence becoming too widely known in Galveston, she figured by now most in the office knew of it anyway. "Certainly," she replied.

Bark provided introductions to a dozen or more Starbuck employees, including the red-haired clerk who had greeted them when they entered.

By the time Jessie and Ki exited the office and turned

onto the street toward the hotel, it was late afternoon and the buildings cast long shadows across the street. Activities were slowing down and a cool breeze floated in off the Gulf. Jessie was tired, and thought how good it would be to get a full night's sleep in a fine bed.

Ki had an uneasy feeling, one that he had not been able to shake since he'd arrived on Galveston Island. Maybe it was the sinister presence of Lord Clinton Bly, or maybe it was those lingering thoughts that perhaps Wade Shaw had been correct and that Jessie was indeed in danger from The Scorpion.

Too, while standing at the window in Bark's office, Ki thought he had spotted the evil man with the eye patch that he and Jessie had noticed in the train station. Maybe it was all coincidence as Jessie had suggested earlier, but Ki's instinct said nothing in life was purely coincidence, that everything had a reason in the great unseen scheme of being.

"Marty's a good man," Jessie said as they walked.

Ki ignored her. He was deep in thought, trying to ease his worries. They crossed the street that ran beside the hotel, turned at the corner, and started approaching the stable.

Ki had gone no more than two steps, when he saw him.

It was the man with the eye patch!

Ki's muscles tightened. Was he imagining or had he actually seen the man's head peek out from the stable alley?

Jessie sensed something amiss. "What is it?"

"I don't know," Ki replied. "Maybe our one-eyed friend again." He held up his hand and stopped Jessie. Both stood listening. Then they heard the sound of a commotion from the alley, then the sound of a woman's cries. "It could be a trick," Ki said, starting to run for the alley, Jessie following him.

Ki jumped into the alley and assessed what he could see in the deep shadows. Four men—including Eye Patch—halfway down the alley were attempting to beat a slight man and a dark-haired woman in a colorful dress.

"Your money," shouted one.

"Come on, let's go," cried Eye Patch. "Here comes someone."

The three men working over the couple forgot them for a moment and spun around. "Hell, we can beat him too," one of them said.

Ki charged down the alley.

Eye Patch retreated behind the other three and bent over and tried to pull the wallet from the male victim's coat. The three remaining robbers ran to confront Ki.

When they were within striking distance, Ki loosed a flying kick that caught the first one in the jaw and rattled his teeth. He went sprawling to the ground, cursing and flailing at air.

The next one pulled a knife, but Ki spun around and kicked it from his hand, then grabbed his arm and flipped him on his back. He landed with a groan, too stunned to get up for a moment.

The third one came at him with a club and swung it at Ki's head. Ki ducked, then charged past this assailant and spun around. When the ruffian turned to face Ki, the *ninja* charged, then flew feet-first into the ruffian's stomach. The club went flying and the assailant fell to the ground, gasping for breath.

Ki twisted around to take on Eye Patch, but he retreated to where the alley turned to exit on the back street.

"Come on," Eye Patch yelled.

The three Ki had downed managed to get up, then started toward Jessie, who stood with her feet planted in the alleyway and her hands holding the derringer she carried in her garter holster.

Ki scurried to the downed couple, quickly helping them up and herding them against the wall in case Jessie shot.

The three men stopped, then turned around and raced back down the alley toward Ki and the couple he had saved.

Ki shielded the couple as the three stumbled by, mumbling in pain or cursing. Like Eye Patch they escaped out the back alley.

Lowering her gun hand, Jessie ran to Ki. "I couldn't shoot with you behind them."

Ki nodded, then turned around to the couple he had saved from the ruffians. The middle-aged man bent over and picked up a top hat, then began brushing it off as he straightened back up. He was a slender man, barely five feet, four inches tall, but nattily attired. Then Ki glanced at the woman and caught his breath. Before him stood as beautiful a creature as he had ever seen. He knew by her sallow skin, the slant of her eyes, and the black hair tied in a bun behind her head she was the offspring of Japanese parents. Ki just stared, stunned by her beauty. She seemed to realize the effect she was having on him, and she seemed both pleased and embarrassed. Ki stood awkwardly silent, his gaze fixed upon the young woman, who wore a dress of the flowery silk favored by her people, but cut in a European rather than Asian style.

Ki was relieved when Jessie spoke because his tongue seemed suddenly paralyzed.

"Are you hurt, either of you?" she asked.

"I think not, good lady and good sir," the man answered with a flourish as he replaced his top hat over his thinning hair. He wore a silk suit, fancy shirt, and diamond stick pin in a silk cravat. His shoes were polished to a high shine that gave a reflection like a mirror of the finest glass. He bent over and picked up a cane with a golden leaping lion for a handle.

Ki studied the young Japanese woman, who was maybe half her companion's age. She avoided his direct glance, but he could see she was intrigued by him.

"The pair of you, good lady and good sir, saved myself and my assistant considerable money and perhaps even our lives. I should like to reward you handsomely for your bravery." His hand reached inside his coat pocket and withdrew a thick wallet. He opened it and thumbed the bills inside. Ki saw bills in hundred- and thousand-dollar denominations and little else.

81

Jessie held up her hand. "That is not necessary. We don't need your money."

The man shook his head. "You Texans, good lady, are a proud, stubborn brood, though I am not at all certain your companion is Texan. I insist that you accept my generosity. I assure you that it is but a pittance to me and I assure you that I get what I want."

Jessie shook her head. "Your thanks is plenty."

The man snapped the wallet shut. "Then at least allow me to have the honor, good lady and good sir, of treating you to as fine a dinner as money can buy. That would be but a token of my gratitude to the pair of you."

"That is more to our liking," Jessie replied.

"Superior," replied the man. "Allow me to introduce ourselves. This is my assistant, Mai Lay, and I am Lord Clinton Bly."

★

Chapter 10

This small man was Lord Clinton Bly? Jessie could not believe it. Bly was the governor's size. She had expected a man as big and threatening as his reputation, but Lord Bly was a little man. Jessie smiled to cover what must surely be the surprise in her face and eyes. She extended her hand. "Lord Bly," she announced, "I am Jessica Starbuck."

Lord Bly seemed as startled by her announcement as she'd been by his. His mouth dropped and he turned to Mai Lay, who bowed her head subserviently to him. Lord Bly doffed his hat. "Miss Starbuck, it is indeed an honor to make your acquaintance. I had heard you had arrived in town and had planned to introduce myself formally at the appropriate time." After replacing his hat, he took Jessie's proffered hand and shook it delicately, as if it might break. Gently, he released her hand.

"I must thank you for your generous gesture of vacating the Grand Suite for me," Jessie said.

Lord Bly tapped his cane. "Adequate, perhaps, but never grand, the suite. My ship quarters are much more commodious. No offense, Miss Starbuck, about the hotel."

"Not at all, and please call me Jessie." She turned to Mai Lay and offered her hand.

Bly's assistant hesitated, then looked to Bly, who answered with a slight nod. Mai Lay bowed to Jessie, then meekly took her hand.

"I would like the two of you to meet my assistant, Ki," said Jessie.

Lord Bly nodded at Ki, but did not lift his hand to seal the introduction. Mai Lay, though, quickly offered Ki her hand. She seemed to quiver at his touch, and Jessie could see that Ki was taken with Mai Lay.

"The invitation to dinner still stands," Bly said, motioning to the street with his cane. "I would feel better out in the open rather than in this queer passage where those brigands forced us."

Bly offered Jessie his arm. She slipped hers in his and moved toward the street and the dwindling afternoon light. Glancing over her shoulder, Jessie saw Ki offer Mai Lay his arm. She bowed meekly to him, then slid her arm in his to follow. Barely over five feet tall, she made an amusing partner with Ki, who was more than a head taller.

At the sidewalk, Jessie pulled her arm from Bly's. "I should be pleased to have dinner with you on two conditions."

"Relate them to me," answered Bly, sliding his cane under his shoulder.

She smiled as Ki and Mai Lay stopped beside them. "First, that Ki and Mai Lay join us for dinner."

"Acceptable, good lady, acceptable," replied Bly.

"And," continued Jessie, "that we discuss no business tonight."

Bly pulled his cane from beneath his shoulder and held it with both hands at his waist. "You have my word, Miss Starbuck, but I must warn you of one thing."

"Which is?"

"That I am not nearly as bad as my reputation." Bly punctuated his warning with a disarming laugh.

"Then we shall have a good dinner," Jessie said.

"Shall we meet at eight o'clock?" Bly asked.

"That would be fine. Say the lobby of the hotel?"

"Acceptable."

"And I would suggest we dine in the Crown Hotel. The restaurant is superb."

"As long as I am allowed to buy as a small token of my appreciation for your bravery, the restaurant is your choice. We shall see you at eight o'clock. Come along, Mai Lay," said Lord Bly, and the odd pair turned back down the walk for Bly's yacht.

Jessie and Ki stood silent, watching them turn the corner.

"Some coincidence," Jessie said as they disappeared from sight.

For the first time since his gaze fell upon Mai Lay, Ki was able to speak. "Nothing is coincidence in life. Everything follows a certain plan, a certain order of nature."

"She's a beautiful woman." Jessie looked at Ki and could see his discomfort. He was taken by her, Jessie could tell, but Jessie knew that he had vowed to protect *her* for life. He was totally devoted to guarding Jessie, and he believed that any emotional attachment to another woman would lessen his devotion to Jessie and demean his lifetime vow.

"And he's a powerful man, maybe too powerful," Ki observed.

They turned and walked silently to the front of the Crown Hotel, standing for a moment under the portico, silently contemplating their encounter with the fearsome Lord Clinton Bly.

Jessie finally turned to Ki. "Perhaps we should go to our rooms and rest. We've a couple hours, Ki, and I should inform the desk clerk to have some formal clothes brought to our rooms for proper dinner attire tonight."

Ki seemed more inscrutable than ever, and Jessie wished for once that she could read his mind. They entered the hotel, Jessie relaying instructions at the desk for the clothes to be delivered to their suites. The clerk gave Jessie and Ki keys to their new suites.

They climbed the stairs together, then unlocked the doors to their adjoining suites.

"We shall go down together precisely at eight," Jessie said.

Ki nodded as Jessie entered and locked the door behind her. Lord Clinton Bly's assessment aside, the Grand Suite was a fine suite, with a comfortable drawing room with thick carpet and furniture of fine mahogany and plush velvet upholstery. Beyond the drawing room was a large bedroom with a thick mattress and silk sheets. To one side of the bedroom was a large bathroom with a marble tub and running hot and cold water. On the other side of the bedroom was a large closet. The bedroom led out onto the balcony atop the carriage portico.

Jessie strode into the bedroom and stopped in surprise. A huge bouquet of flowers stood on the table at the foot of the large bed. She approached the bouquet in awe. It was as big as a steamer trunk. Seeing a card peeking from between the colorful roses, she plucked it from among the petals and opened the envelope. She pulled out a card and read it aloud. "To our mutual business interests. Lord Clinton Bly."

Shaking her head, Jessie felt amused by Bly's smooth efforts to win her over. He was trying to set her up to get his way. Jessie knew she would not be swayed by sentimentality, even if some women were. After all, her good business sense was what kept the Starbuck empire thriving, that and her ability to keep good managers like Martin Bark.

Jessie looked about the room as she strolled toward the balcony. Everything was in order except the closet door was slightly ajar. It was a small detail that might have been overlooked in Lord Clinton Bly's quick departure or when the maid had moved her new clothes from her previous suite to this one.

The room was perfumed with the aroma of the flowers, and Jessie pulled a rose from the bouquet and strolled toward the windows overlooking the balcony. She drew back the floor-length drapes that covered the windows, then opened the narrow door that led outside. The balcony was wide, and shared not only by Jessie's suite but by Ki's as well.

She stood for several minutes watching a pastel sky grow slowly darker and darker. She sniffed at the rose she carried and enjoyed the spring coolness of the ocean breeze. Thinking she might rest a few minutes, she slipped back in the room. She moved to close the drapes so she could undress and rest.

As she reached for the drape pull, she realized something was amiss. The closet door was not just ajar, it was wide open now!

She reached for her pocket, where she had slipped her derringer after the incident by the stable, but before she could reach it, a hand slipped out from behind the drapes to grab her wrist and another hand appeared to cover her mouth before she could scream.

Jessie panicked for an instant as strong hands and arms tightened their grip around her. She felt a body pressing against her back and then the warm breath of her captor upon her neck. She shuddered, then stiffened at the sound of a raspy voice.

"Are you ready, Jessica Starbuck, to see the face of The Scorpion?"

Trying to stall for time enough to collect her wits, Jessie gave no answer.

"If so," continued the voice, which began to lose its raspiness, "then you better not go anywhere without me as your bodyguard."

Jessie relaxed at the words of Wade Shaw. His hand slid from her mouth and her wrist as he spun her around to face him. She couldn't help but smile. She was glad to see him and not too angry at his trick, though she had to pretend to be for a moment.

As he moved his lips toward hers, Jessie lifted the rose in her other hand between them and Wade Shaw kissed the flower instead.

He jerked his head back, as his hand flew to his cheek. "No call for that," he said. "A damn thorn pricked my cheek."

Jessie backed away from him and tossed the rose on the bed.

The Texas Ranger looked longingly from Jessie to the bed.

"No cause for you sneaking up on me and scaring me out of my wits," Jessie said, knowing that had Shaw taken any longer to identify himself, he might well have wound up with her heel in his groin.

"Just to prove a point, Jessie," Shaw replied. "You need more than Ki around to protect you."

Jessie tossed her head so that her copper-blond tresses bounced seductively on her shoulders. "You're right," she whispered.

Shaw flinched in surprise that she agreed with his comment.

"I need more than Ki right now, but it's not protection I need." With the tip of her tongue, she licked her lips. Shaw's grin grew as big as the sudden bulge in his jeans.

She began to unbutton her high-top blouse beneath her jacket. One, two, three, four buttons came free and the vee of the material plunged toward the vee of her breasts. Buttons five, six, seven, eight, and nine came undone and her blouse was open, her breasts pressing against the edge of the material. With the grace of a swan, Jessie slowly lowered the blouse and jacket from her shoulders, more and more of her breasts emerging as an open invitation to Shaw.

And yet Shaw stood still, never making a move toward her, just watching her slow ritual. That was one thing she liked about the Texas Ranger. He was patient and went about his lovemaking with deliberation, instead of the haste valued by less disciplined men.

Jessie pulled her blouse from her skirt, then placed it and her jacket on the bed. She lifted each foot and removed her shoes, then slid her skirt from her waist, stopping when a patch of the golden fleece between her thighs came into view.

Wade Shaw bit his lip as he stared and let his hand brush against the front of his jeans.

To tease him, she pulled the skirt back up.

He took a step toward her.

Jessie shoved her skirt down past her thighs, and it fell the rest of the way to the floor.

Shaw stopped and shook his head in admiration. "You're beautiful, Jessie, every bit of you." His gaze seemed to bound back and forth from her lips to her breasts and to the downy triangle between her legs.

Jessie let herself gently down upon the bed beside the discarded rose. She opened her legs to him and he bit his lip again.

Slowly, he began to undress, teasing her as she had teased him. He removed his gunbelt, then his shirt, then his boots and jeans, and was finally naked, his body as firm and hard as his desire.

For a moment, he stood at attention before her, giving Jessie a moment to enjoy what would soon be hers. Then he stepped softly to the bed, not in the rush of less disciplined men, but with the patience of a caring lover. As he reached the mattress, he picked up the rose, then slid into bed beside her.

Jessie reached up to meet him and to pull his desire toward her, but he pushed away her hand. Jessie moaned, first in frustration because she was aching so for him, and then in pleasure as he took the rose and began to brush the tip of its soft head against her nipples. The touch of the rose was as soft as an angel's kiss when he began to stroke her nipples and then her breasts in ever-widening circles. Jessie arched her back, thrusting her breasts toward him, hoping he would grab or kiss them. Instead, he kept exploring her with the rose, gradually working his way down to her navel and then to the fleece that clothed her womanly folds of flesh.

She moaned and cried out, "Please, now." But the rose merely passed the inviting wetness and stroked the soft flesh of her inner thighs.

"Are you glad to see me?" he teased.

Jessie shook her head and bucked her body, desirous not only of seeing him, but feeling his manliness within her.

Gently, he placed the rose upon the golden fleece between her legs, then leaned over and kissed her full on the mouth. She lifted to meet his lips, pressing hers hard against him. As she answered his kiss, she felt his hand slide from her cheek down her neck to her breasts. She gasped in pleasure as he lightly squeezed each nipple between his fingers, then kneaded each breast.

He broke his lips from hers, then moved his mouth to her breast. Again she arched her back to lift her breasts for him. She gasped as he took one breast, then the other in his mouth. Shaw's wandering hand continued its delicate descent down her body, softly stroking her stomach, then knocking the rose from her pubis and grabbing her firmly with his hand.

At his touch the flame of passion that had warmed the spot between her legs erupted like molten lava and she thrashed against him. Until then she had wanted to pleasure him as he had pleasured her, but now she no longer cared. She just wanted satisfaction.

"Please," she begged, and he delayed. She flung her fists against his chest and pushed him over until he was sprawled on his back. Then she climbed atop him, straddling his ripened manliness. She pushed down against him, but he dodged her thrust.

She glanced down into his dark eyes, which smiled like his lips. She loved him and hated him all at once for his teasing. She tried again and he dodged her move.

He grabbed her breasts and squeezed them softly. "Only when you do it slowly," he said.

Jessie sighed, took a deep breath, then took him inside herself. She rocked gently upon him, her knees bent and straddling his strong, powerful hips. The animal in her wanted to thrash against Wade Shaw's stiff desire, but when she tried, he pulled away from her to slow the pace.

Whenever she managed the perfect pace, Wade Shaw would take his hands and fondle her breasts. She enjoyed the touch of him on her bosom while she squeezed him between her legs. Ten, fifteen, twenty minutes went by, and she lost all track of time and of everything else except the desire within her.

Then, Wade Shaw began to pant and his eyes began to widen. He arched his back to meet her thrusts, and she screamed in delight as he began to rock harder and harder against her until they both let out a simultaneous scream and she collapsed on his chest, covering his face with kisses and receiving the same from him.

He wrapped his arms around her back and squeezed her tightly. "It's better that way," he said.

"You're right." Jessie sighed as she felt his spent passion between her thighs.

She could have stayed in his arms forever, except for a knock on the door.

"Maid," said the voice. "I've the seamstress with fancy dresses for you."

"I'm not dressed," Jessie said, "just let yourself in and leave them in the drawing room for me to select."

"Yes, ma'am," the maid replied. In a moment, Jessie heard the door open and the rustle of lace and silk dresses being placed upon the furniture in the adjacent room. "Thank you, ma'am," said the unseen voice.

"What time is it?" Jessie asked the maid.

"Quarter of eight," the maid replied as the door shut and the key locked the room again.

"A quarter of eight?" Jessie bounced up from bed like a whirlwind. "I've got to get dressed for a dinner."

"What?" Shaw called. "I don't get more?"

Jessie groaned as she ran to the bathroom to sponge off, then rushed into the front room to check out the dresses that had been brought. She hoped one would fit and accentuate her figure for Shaw.

"Who are you having dinner with?" Shaw called.

"Ki, Lord Clinton Bly, and his assistant," Jessie answered as she picked up a low-cut yellow dress that she thought would accentuate her bosom and her smooth brown complexion. As she held the dress in front of her, she glanced up to see Wade

Shaw standing at the door wearing nothing but the shirt he was buttoning.

"I'll be dining with you," he announced.

"You're not invited," Jessie responded.

"My job's to look after you. You heard the governor."

"We're dining downstairs and will not be leaving the hotel."

"No matter, Jessie. I'll be dining with you, whether you like it or not. We've heard The Scorpion is in Texas now, so that's one reason I'll be shadowing you, for your own good. Second thing, before all this came up I was trying to break a gun-smuggling ring that is supplying weapons to Mexico, fomenting revolution."

Jessie stepped into the long dress and pulled it up to her waist, then slid her arms in the sleeve openings and pulled the top over her breasts. She adjusted her bosom in the dress, then tried to button up the back. "So what's gun smuggling got to do with me?" she replied, angered that she was unable to fix the top buttons without Shaw's help.

"Nothing with you, Jessie."

She turned around placed her hands on the curves of her hips. "Are you gonna help or not?"

Shaw eased over behind her and started buttoning the back of the dress. "Gun smuggling has nothing to do with you, but Lord Clinton Bly is going from here to Mexico."

"He's trying to corner the cotton market," Jessie replied.

After fastening the last button, Shaw gave Jessie a gentle swat on the fanny. Jessie scurried out of the drawing room into the bathroom, picking up a brush and running it through her hair.

Shaw followed her to the bathroom door. "Could be cotton's his game, then maybe not. A shipment of guns may be coming here by train from New Orleans. He's going to Mexico. Seems to me this is more than just a coincidence."

Jessie scurried past Shaw, glancing about for her shoes. She found them by the bed and slipped the right one on.

Even though they didn't match, they would be hidden by the long dress.

"Coincidence!" Jessie exclaimed. "If I hear that word mentioned one more time today, I think I'll scream." She stamped her foot on the carpet as she tried to get her left foot to slide into its shoe.

"It's about eight," Shaw said. As he lifted his arms, his spent manhood peeked from between the pleats at the base of his shirt. "You're gonna be late."

"Thanks to you!" she shot back as she ran her fingers through her hair a final time.

"You're welcome," he answered.

Jessie groaned as she started for the door, totally exasperated by this intriguing man.

"I'll be joining you in the restaurant shortly," he said.

"Don't forget your pants," she said before opening the door and emerging into the hall where Ki stood waiting.

Ki just shook his head.

★

Chapter 11

As Jessie and Ki marched down the stairs, Lord Clinton Bly and Mai Lay entered the lobby. Bly wore a black top hat, cutaway coat, striped trousers, and a white shirt, tie, and gloves. He toted the same cane he had carried earlier.

Jessie had to admit Mai Lay was stunning. She wore a white sarong dress that funneled down to her ankles. When she took her tiny steps, the slit in the dress exposed the striking flesh of her calf. Above the dress's high neck, her face was powdered and rouged like a geisha's and her eyes were dark and intriguing. Her black hair was layered in progressively smaller buns, each adorned with tiny flowers. When Mai Lay saw Ki, she lifted her hand and spread apart a Japanese fan to shield her face.

As Ki took in Mai Lay he seemed to straighten his shoulders even more than normal. Out of the corner of her eye, Jessie thought she saw a trace of a smile on Ki's thin lips.

At her approach, Lord Clinton Bly doffed his top hat and snapped his heels together as he offered a nod of his head. "Good evening, good lady," he said. "You look ravishing," he said, extending his hand for hers.

Jessie couldn't help but laugh to herself at the remembrance of how little time she had spent dressing. But then again, she knew this was Bly's game of flattery to win her over so she would listen to and ultimately accept his business offer. She offered him her hand and he lifted it to his lips to kiss it.

Releasing her hand, he turned to Ki. "Good evening, Mr. Ki. By your clothes I see you must know of the best draper's shop in Galveston. Would you mind escorting Mai Lay for the evening? She is a delicate flower, unwise in the customs of Europe and America, but an unquestioning and loyal assistant who can be trusted with the most secret of my business plans."

"My pleasure, Lord Bly," Ki replied.

"Indeed it can be, Mr. Ki," Bly said matter-of-factly. "Mai Lay is a master of the Japanese carnal arts."

Mai Lay looked up at Ki, her dark sensual eyes just visible over the top of her fan. Ki took her arm in his and turned her toward the glass and mahogany door that opened into the restaurant.

Lord Bly took Jessie's arm and escorted her inside. They were shown to a corner table and Lord Bly ordered the most expensive wine. After toasting Ki for his fancy handling of the would-be robbers, Bly signaled for the waiter, a tall, slender man with blond hair and blue eyes. The waiter presented the menu.

Bly insisted on turtle soup all around and lobster salad to begin the meal, then ordered stuffed partridge with asparagus for himself. Jessie requested turkey *aux truffes* and *chouxfleurs au beurre,* while Ki and Mai Lay settled on broiled redfish with cabbage sprouts.

More than anything else, Ki and Mai Lay had settled on each other, Jessie thought as she watched them. There was a quiet magnetism between them that drew them and their whispers closer to one another. Their whispering was unnecessary because they spoke their secrets in Japanese.

The waiter had just removed the soup bowls and brought the lobster salad when Jessie saw Wade Shaw being seated at a table across the room. He offered her a sly grin as if he knew his presence annoyed her. She kept glancing intermittently from her salad to Wade Shaw while Lord Bly spoke.

"Excellent salad," he concluded. "Much better than anything I expected in this obscure port."

There was a pause. Jessie realized too late that Lord Bly had expected an answer. He looked from Jessie to Wade Shaw. "That man, good lady, is he bothering you? I can pay him to depart."

Jessie shook her head. "He's too stubborn, the type that can't be bought."

"And what's his business with you?"

"A Texas Ranger. The governor assigned him to guard me."

Lord Bly raised his dark eyebrows. "The governor of Texas, am I right?"

Jessie nodded.

"But why?"

"It's a foolish reason."

"Surely your governor is not a fool?"

"He's a politician," replied Jessie. "He got word that some assassin was stalking me."

"Good God, no," Bly shouted, lifting his napkin to his lips and patting them nervously.

"An assassin called The Scorpion."

Bly's mouth dropped, and Mai Lay turned her head from Ki to Jessie.

With narrowed eyes, Ki too stared at Jessie, and she knew she had made a mistake in mentioning The Scorpion, but now it was too late. Bly seemed shocked by the revelation. "You've heard of this man?" Jessie asked.

Bly shook his head. "Europe's most feared assassin. No one knows what he looks like, just that he's deadly successful. I am glad the governor has seen fit to assign someone to guard you. Shall I invite him to join us?"

"Oh, no," replied Jessie, "let him watch from afar."

"Very well then, good lady, but let me assure you that if

you feel in any danger you can call upon the full measure of my resources worldwide," Bly offered.

"Thank you. Now, you were speaking about the lobster salad," Jessie said.

"Yes, much better than I anticipated."

"I think you will say the same of all the food here."

Though they had resumed their conversation, Ki and Mai Lay seemed more on guard now than they had been before Jessie had mentioned The Scorpion.

The waiter brought the main course and the four dined leisurely. True to his promise, Lord Clinton Bly did not once mention business. As the waiter cleared their empty plates from the table, Bly said something that made Jessie straighten in her seat.

"I had the occasion to once meet your father. Alex Starbuck was a fine man, a man I looked up to." Bly chuckled. "I look up to most men at my height, but he was one whom I admired. By his ironclad will and integrity he gained what most men desire; wealth, renown, and a beautiful woman like your mother. I compare what I wish to be with what your father was, but unfortunately I do not have his talents and, alas, do not meet his standard."

Mention of her father brought a lump to Jessie's throat, and she felt that Lord Clinton Bly, by baring his own shortcomings, was extending to her father the greatest compliment a man could give. "I am honored you thought so highly of my father."

"What he did in beginning the destruction of the cartel and what you did in finishing its demise deserves the world's undying gratitude," Bly continued. "I say this, good lady, so that you will understand that my methods of business will vary from your father's but my goal is very much the same as his—to make this a better world for us all."

For a brief instant, Jessie thought she saw the glimmer of a tear in Lord Bly's eye as the waiter appeared.

"Now, waiter," Bly said, "we are ready for dessert."

The waiter presented the dessert menu.

"As host," announced Bly, "I should like to pick the dessert for this evening. Please, serve us all raisin *de cassis* and macaroons. And waiter," said Bly, pointing to Wade Shaw, "please provide the Texas Ranger the same dessert and inform him I will be glad to pick up his check as a token of my appreciation for his service to the law of Texas and for his protection of my beautiful guest."

The waiter returned shortly with a tray of desserts for Bly's table, then took a serving as well to Wade Shaw. Jessie smiled at the Ranger as the waiter approached his table, then felt her grin wilt as Shaw refused Bly's simple gesture.

For a moment, the waiter stood frozen, then turned and reluctantly walked back to Bly's table. The waiter cleared his throat, then grimaced. "The gentleman declines your offer, saying he would rather pay for it himself."

Shaw slowly nodded to Bly to confirm the waiter's words.

"Such a pity," responded Bly, "that a man who will not make in a lifetime what I will make in an hour has such a stubborn pride. He may be many things as a Texas Ranger, but rich will never be one of them."

Jessie stared hard at Wade Shaw, embarrassed at his manners. "I will apologize for him."

"Indeed not. If a man makes his cup of tea, then he should drink it himself."

As they finished dessert, Bly turned to Jessie. "Tomorrow Mai Lay and I have planned a little expedition on the island. We would like you and Mr. Ki to join us."

"What kind of expedition?"

Bly looked all around, his gaze lingering on Wade Shaw for a moment. Then he leaned closer to Jessie. "We plan to search for the buried treasure of Jean Lafitte."

Jessie cackled. "You're kidding."

"Do you mean that other famous pirate Captain Kidding?" Bly said, then laughed at his own joke. "Serious? Indeed I am. What could be more fun? I've a couple days in Galveston before I must leave. Plenty of time for us to discuss business, but why not have a tad bit of fun while we are here?"

"We'd be pleased," Jessie answered.

"Splendid," replied Bly. "I'll secure us a pair of carriages and we shall traverse the island until we uncover Lafitte's buried treasure. With luck, we'll be rich by nightfall." Bly laughed at his latest joke. "If we are to be on the prowl by nine, then Mai Lay and I must retire. Do you mind if we call it a night, good lady?"

"Not at all," Jessie replied, glancing over to Ki and Mai Lay, who talked in their hushed Japanese.

"That is why I will rent two carriages tomorrow. One for them and one for us." Bly tapped his finger on the table and Mai Lay looked over immediately to him. "We must be departing."

Mai Lay nodded meekly, then turned to Jessie. She spoke very softly. "I hope I shall see you and Ki again."

"The pleasure was ours," Jessie replied.

Ki helped Mai Lay from her chair and Bly assisted Jessie with hers. Bly removed his wallet from his coat pocket and very deliberately counted out five hundred dollars for Wade Shaw to see. He left the money on the table for the meal and the waiter's gratuity, then smugly put his wallet back in his pocket.

He took Jessie in his arm and steered her by Wade Shaw's table. "I left more on the table than a Texas Ranger makes in a year," he said, loud enough for Shaw to hear.

Jessie cast an angry gaze at Shaw as she passed his table and exited. By the time she had seen Bly and Mai Lay out he door, Shaw was at the foot of the stairs waiting for her. She strode past him and bounded up the steps. He chased after her and quickly caught her as Ki followed casually behind them.

Shaw grabbed Jessie's arm and stopped her at the head of the stairs.

Jessie flew around and slapped him. "I have never been so embarrassed in all my life."

"I don't take charity from a man I don't respect," Shaw said.

"Maybe Bly doesn't deserve your respect, but he does deserve to be treated with whatever manners you possess."

Wearing a smirk on his face, Ki walked past them. "You missed a good dessert, Shaw, and good night," he said as he walked to his room.

"Hell, for all you know, Jessie, he could be The Scorpion."

"For all I know, Wade Shaw, *you* could be The Scorpion." Jessie jerked her arm free and started for her room with Shaw trailing her stride for stride. Jessie stopped and spun around to face him. "Where do you think you are going?"

"To your room, where else?"

"What?"

"I'm under the governor's orders to protect you."

"Then rent a room down the hall."

"My expense money won't cover something as expensive as a room at the Crown."

"You should've thought of that when you insulted Lord Bly's offer to buy your dinner. Then maybe you'd have enough for a room."

"Don't need enough for a room," Shaw replied, "because when the desk clerk wasn't looking, I stole a key to yours."

Jessie reached her door and moved to insert her key in the lock.

Shaw, though, beat her with his own and unlocked the door, shoving it open. "After you," he teased.

Jessie flew through the door, through the drawing room, and into the bedroom.

"You may be sharing my suite, but you'll not share my bed tonight, Wade Shaw."

The Ranger grinned. "I think I've put in a good day's work already."

Jessie shrugged and turned away. She was exasperated with him, and yet even more strongly attracted to him, though she could never let him know that. "You can sleep on the sofa in the drawing room," she told him.

After she undressed and bathed, Jessie stood by the window so he could see her naked body in the moon glow, hoping to tease him into some manners. When she went to bed, she felt strangely secure that he was nearby. Though she wanted him dearly, she knew she should not let him know so easily. She had a fitful time dozing off, especially when she realized by his light snoring that he was having no such difficulty in finding sleep.

★

Chapter 12

"That is our destination," said Lord Clinton Bly, pointing with his right hand while his left held the buggy reins. "The three trees."

"Trees is a generous description," Jessie said with a laugh. "They're more like overgrown shrubs."

"Indeed, good lady, but who knows what you will find on a treasure hunt."

"Most likely, nothing," Jessie replied.

"Like fox hunting, good lady, it's not the thrill of the kill but the thrill of the chase. It's much the same as negotiating a business deal."

Jessie turned away from Lord Clinton Bly. She did not care to discuss business. Despite Martin Bark's warning and Wade Shaw's skepticism of Lord Bly, Jessie found him not nearly so bad as his reputation. She knew she was influenced by his kind words and admiration for her father. Still, maybe Bark and Shaw were right about him and this was all a facade that would change as soon as they got down to business.

"If we find the treasure," Jessie said, "there's no need to discuss business."

"Now, good lady, you are sounding like me." He shook

the reins against the sorrel's rump and the buggy accelerated down the hardpacked trail.

The trail passed through patches of spindly grasses that swayed in the soft breeze. The soil was streaked with splotches of gray, brown, and yellow sand that gave the island an anemic hue. Overhead sea gulls hovered, accustomed to the picnic leftovers of the many islanders who made Sunday expeditions to search for Lafitte's treasure.

Jessie twisted around and looked behind her at the buggy Ki was driving. Ki had fallen behind, but not so far that Jessie couldn't see Mai Lay as close to him as a barnacle on a ship's hull. Mai Lay was good for Ki because she was from the land of his birth, from his culture. Like Ki, she had been pulled away from her heritage. Jessie did not know why, though she hoped not merely to serve as Lord Clinton Bly's concubine. Perhaps Ki could find in Mai Lay the companion that she felt he needed.

Jessie smiled at the thought until she caught a glimpse of Wade Shaw back down the trail, following the buggies. In his arrogance, Shaw had insisted on accompanying Jessie beyond Galveston, which was barely visible behind them. Instead of being a gentleman about it and accepting Jessie's suggestion of riding with them, Shaw had opted to skulk a couple hundred yards behind them, stalking them like a common criminal. For that reason, she was glad to see a picnic basket along with the shovels in the back of Bly's rented buggy. She suspected Bly had plans to stay past lunch, and Shaw had not come prepared for such a contingency. It would serve Shaw right to go hungry for a while because of the embarrassment he was causing her.

As her buggy came within a hundred yards of the three trees, Jessie saw a landscape pitted and pimpled from the diggings of treasure hunters past. The mounds of sand were monuments to their failures. It was foolish to think Bly's luck or her own would be any different, but Jessie did have to admit it was fun to consider the possibility.

"Good lady," offered Bly, "I feel that we are nearing great wealth." He surveyed the pockmarked ground as he reined the sorrel horse and buggy to a stop. "Fools, fools," he shouted to the wind, "anyone can see you've dug in the wrong places." He turned to Jessie. "That is why I brought you, good lady, to bring me the luck the previous fools lacked."

"Good luck," Jessie said dryly.

Bly clapped his gloved hands together. "No, no, good lady. You shall select the site where we shall dig up a fortune."

Jessie laughed. "It's good, Lord Bly, that you are already wealthy because this won't work."

"Indeed it will, good lady." Bly tied the buggy reins, then stood up in the buggy, like a ship's captain surveying the ocean. "Select the spot."

"This is crazy. Anywhere will do."

"No, good lady, I insist that you select a spot."

Jessie refused again.

"You, good lady, are as stubborn as your Texas Ranger friend," Bly said, glancing behind the buggy to check on Shaw's whereabouts.

"Must be the Texan in us."

Bly removed his top hat and gave it to Jessie, just as Ki and Mai Lay arrived behind them. "Hold this."

Jessie took it.

"Now," said Bly, "toss it toward the trees."

"What?"

"Toss it at the trees. I insist. Now."

Jessie stood up on the buggy floorboard, planted her feet, and grabbed the top hat by the curved brim. Then she crossed her right arm to her left side and catapulted the top hat toward the trees. It sailed maybe twenty feet, then tumbled to the ground like a bird shot on the wing. The hat landed upright on a patch of undisturbed soil. "How was that?" she asked.

"We will not know, good lady, until we dig. With your touch and my hat, that's where we shall find Lafitte's gold."

Jessie laughed.

Bly jumped to the ground, landing gracefully on his feet, then scurried around the buggy to assist Jessie. He took her hand and helped her down, then pulled a pair of shovels from beside the picnic basket. He issued one to Jessie and took one for himself, then marched like a soldier to his hat.

"Mr. Ki and Mai Lay," he announced as they stepped down from the buggy, "you are about to witness history. The first joint venture of Starbuck Enterprises and Bly International will uncover the treasure buried here more than a half century ago by the great pirate Jean Lafitte."

Ki and Mai Lay seemed more interested in each other than in Bly's announcements. They ambled away from the buggy and toward the trees.

Bly picked up his hat, plopped it on his head, and began to dig. He made an odd sight in his white gloves, suit, and top hat. By contrast, Jessie had worn a riding outfit of a green tweed jacket and skirt, a pale silk blouse, and a brown Stetson that hung over her back by the leather strand around her neck. She stared for a moment, amused at Bly's exuberant attack upon the ground. "Why not?" she said, finally deciding to join in the fun. She adjusted her hat over her copper-blond hair and pulled leather gloves from the pocket of her riding vest. After tugging the gloves in place, she took the shovel and went to Bly's side.

"Couldn't resist such fun, good lady, could you?"

"Couldn't resist the gold," she said with a laugh.

Together, they began to excavate a broad hole that got bigger and bigger with each spadeful of soil they extracted. It was high fun, except for the occasional glances Jessie got of Wade Shaw making a wide circle around them, their buggies, and their trees. She pulled up shovel after shovel of earth while Bly dug with a maniacal fury, taking up two shovels for every one of hers. He had good wind and strength for such a small man.

After thirty minutes of solid digging, Jessie's energy, if not her spirit, sagged. And at just the moment she thought she should rest, she pressed her boot against the top of the blade and pushed the spade into the ground. It came to a jarring stop against something hard. She giggled with excitement.

She removed a shovelful of dirt, then another, again clunking against an obstacle. "Could it be?"

"Indeed, good lady, I foresaw this would be a lucky endeavor." He did a little jig as he moved from his location to hers. Standing opposite her, he began to dig in Jessie's direction. Then his shovel hit something hard as well. "I suspect it's wood." He paused for a moment to take off his coat, throwing it aside as he grabbed the shovel and attacked the growing pit.

Gradually, they uncovered a curve of dark, damp wood.

"A treasure chest," Jessie shouted as her shovel uncovered more of the buried object.

They exposed a wooden top, then dug beside it. Though the ends were flat, the sides were curved. The more of the object they uncovered the less it looked like a treasure chest.

"It's a barrel." Jessie frowned.

"Indeed it is, good lady," Bly said without missing a beat in the steady rhythm of his excavation. "If you were burying treasure, would you rather put it in a perfectly fine chest or in an empty barrel?"

Jessie grinned, and began to attack the earth packed around the barrel. Gradually, they uncovered it. Bly kicked the barrel, but it failed to budge. He worked his shovel beneath it and pulled down on the handle, trying to get enough leverage to budge it, but the ground was too soft for his shovel to take hold. Throwing down her shovel, Jessie climbed down around the barrel and stood with Bly in the shallow pit. Together, they pushed at it with their feet. It didn't budge.

Bly speared the ground with his shovel and clapped his hands, his white gloves now stained with mud. In their euphoria, Bly and Jessie forgot their reserve and their clothes, leaning with their bodies against the barrel, futilely trying to make it move.

"It's filled with something," Bly shouted gleefully.

"Something heavy," cried Jessie.

"Like gold or silver," Bly answered. "Stand back, good lady." Bly jerked his shovel from the ground and lifted it over his head.

Jessie looked around and saw Wade Shaw sitting on his horse less than twenty yards away. The Ranger leaned forward in the saddle, his hands crossed over the saddlehorn as he studied the excitement. In the shade of one of the three trees, Ki and Mai Lay had spread a blanket, and seemed far more interested in each other than the treasure hunt.

"Let's see what's inside," shouted Bly as he swung the shovel from the sky at the barrel. The metal blade hit with a dull thud. Again and again he pounded at the soft wood, occasionally clanging against the iron hoop. Finally, he chipped out enough wood that he could slip his blade under the iron hoop and slide it free of the barrel. As he did, the barrel seemed to expand from the pressure of its load inside.

Jessie caught her breath. She thought she could see the dull gray of metal. Was it silver?

Bly cocked the shovel over his head again, then swung the spade in a powerful arc toward the barrel. The wooden staves split and the end of the barrel collapsed behind the weight of thousands of pieces of metal.

Jessie screamed with excitement and Bly danced another jig for just an instant. Then their mirth sagged like their spirits.

"Nails," said Jessie, "a barrel of nails."

Bly scowled, then bent down and grabbed his shovel, flinging it a dozen yards. "Maybe they should change Lafitte's name to Captain Kidder." He began to snicker, then laugh.

Jessie fought a laugh until a cackle escaped her lips. Then they both started laughing uproariously.

"What is the exchange rate on nails?" Bly said. "If they're worth their weight in gold, we're rich."

Jessie looked at his dirty clothes and his blackened

gloves, then at her own mud-stained outfit. "Filthy rich," she shouted.

They both laughed harder yet.

In her mirth, Jessie took a perverse pleasure in seeing Wade Shaw straighten in his saddle and continue riding circles around them and their buggies.

"Enough excitement for one morning," announced Lord Bly. "Shall we have lunch? I say we shall." Bly brushed at the dirt on his shirt, but his soiled gloves only smeared the smudges. He laughed, then marched to the buggy and retrieved the picnic basket. He carried it to the blanket Ki and Mai Lay had spread in the narrow shade of one of the trees. They excused themselves to walk around together, as if they were in a world of their own.

Bly opened the picnic basket and pulled out a bottle of fine wine and two crystal wine glasses. As he uncorked the bottle, Jessie fished out a small wheel of cheese, hard bread, crackers, boiled eggs, pickles, olives, and a dish of thickly sliced smoked turkey.

After pouring wine, Bly handed Jessie a glass. "To a treasure hunt I'll not soon forget." They clinked glasses and drank, then began to dine on the foods that had been prepared by Bly's chef on the yacht. It was delicious, and there was more than enough for them all. Lord Bly even suggested inviting Wade Shaw to join them, but Jessie tried to discourage him. Ignoring Jessie, Bly jumped up from his blanket and signaled for Shaw to ride in. "You're welcome to dine with us," he called.

Shaw just shook his head and kept on riding. Jessie glared at the Ranger.

"Unsociable chap, your Ranger friend."

"A stubborn mule," Jessie replied.

They stayed until mid-afternoon, then gathered what food they didn't toss to the gulls and started back for Galveston, the vigilant Shaw still trailing them like a buzzard.

As they neared the edge of town, Bly turned to Jessie. "Though my fun has been considerable today, I came here

108

for business and must turn to business, good lady."

Jessie wondered if she would have a less flattering opinion of Lord Clinton Bly once he finished. "Go ahead."

"I seek suppliers of cotton in the States. You control the majority of all cotton shipped out of Texas. I desire some mutually beneficial arrangement allowing me to purchase all of your cotton."

"You can purchase as much of my cotton now as you like, if the price is right." This was where the catch would be, Jessie thought, but she was surprised by his answer.

"Precisely. So I would like for you to consider a price that is amenable to you and your people, a price well above the market value, then join me for dinner aboard the yacht for further discussions." Bly looked back over his shoulder at the trailing buggy. "Mr. Ki can certainly join us."

Jessie was unsure what to say. She had expected him to reveal a scheme to fix prices so he could control the marketplace. Instead, he was willing to discuss a price of her choice. There still had to be a catch somewhere. "Lord Bly, you surprise me."

"I am a man of many surprises. Take Mai Lay, for instance. She is a beautiful woman, some even think a courtesan for me, but she is much more valuable to me than simple carnal purposes. She has a shrewd mind, and when she sits in with me to discuss business with captains of world industry, they are distracted by her beauty and the gossip of her relationship with me. Mai Lay is my protector in a business sense, much as Mr. Ki looks after you. Some men say women, most especially a Japanese woman, have no place in business and resent me because I employ her. These men spread vulgar rumors about me."

"Your reputation is not the best," Jessie replied, still skeptical.

"As I mentioned last night, I am not your father, nor do I have his business acumen or his unquestioned honesty, but I respect those who respect me and abhor those who abhor me. It is the way I am, and I can change it no more than you can

109

change the green of your eyes or the yellow of your hair."

This man still confounded her. He was not like his reputation. She was perplexed by him as they rode through the streets of Galveston, winding up under the carriage portico of the Crown Hotel.

Lord Clinton Bly tipped his dirty hat to Jessie as people on the walk pointed at his filthy clothes. "I shall send Mai Lay for you at eight and we shall dine again together tonight."

Jessie stepped down from the buggy.

"And, good lady, this evening I must insist that we discuss business over dinner."

"As you wish," Jessie responded as a courtesy. Behind her, Jessie watched Ki halt the buggy, then help Mai Lay down. He escorted her to Lord Clinton Bly's rig and helped her in. "I will insist, however," Jessie went on, "that Ki and Mai Lay be allowed to join us for dinner."

"Certainly," Bly replied. "And Mr. Ki, please see that your buggy is returned to the Crown's stables. We will return this rig tonight." Bly rattled the reins, and the buggy moved from under the portico and headed down the street toward the docks and Bly's yacht.

As the buggy turned the corner, Jessie studied Ki, wishing she could read his thoughts as well as he could sometimes read hers. But she could decipher nothing of his thoughts or his emotions. "You seem to like Mai Lay."

"We have much in common," he answered, revealing little of his feelings for the woman.

"Are you fond of her?"

Ki's dark eyes stared into Jessie's. "I have dedicated my life to your service, in honor of your father's kindness to me. She has changed nothing."

Sometimes Jessie hated his stoicism, his unwillingness to be open with her. Her affection for him was a sister's for her brother, and yet though he offered her his total protective devotion, sometimes Jessie wished he would return her genuine affection.

Her concern for Ki was drowned in anger when she saw

110

Wade Shaw ride up, dismount, and walk his horse under the shade of the carriage portico. Jessie abandoned Ki and strode to the Ranger, lifting her finger at his nose. "You are the most pigheaded man I've ever been around."

He grabbed her hand and jerked her to him. "And I'm gonna stay around you until we find The Scorpion." He dropped her hand, then stood with his hands on his hips, devouring her with his eyes. "You need a bath. Need any help?"

She jerked her hand free and hit him with her balled fist. "You're hopeless."

"Me? What about you, spending all day wallowing in the mud with Lord Clinton Bly? I've got more sense than that."

"It didn't keep you from following us and wasting your day."

Shaw shrugged. "I'm just doing my job. What's your excuse?"

Jessie could hear her voice rising. "I'd rather be back on the ranch, working cattle. As long as the governor thought that wasn't wise, I decided I'd attend to some business. I'd feel better about it if you would mind your own business."

Shaw laughed. "My business is minding other people's business, in this instance yours."

Jessie spun around and marched toward Ki. "I've got a bath to take."

"I'll join you once I put up my horse," Shaw said.

Jessie stopped in her tracks. "No, you won't." She felt the exasperation building as she turned back to face him. "You, you . . ."

He dangled his own key to her suite from his fingers. "I'll let myself in."

★

Chapter 13

Wade Shaw led his rented horse to the stable at the back of the Crown Hotel, then retraced his steps to the front, taking enough time to give Jessie a chance to get in the tub. He wasn't sure why he deviled Jessie so, just that he had never met a woman like her. She was certainly beautiful, but so were other women. Jessie, though, had intelligence and a strong will that at times made her a bit headstrong, but that attracted him to her even more. On top of that, Jessie had faced the many bad men in the cartel and had survived. She had the courage and the judgment to be a Texas Ranger. That was what made her a challenge. She was an independent woman. For Shaw, she was the challenge of riding a horse that had never been ridden, roping a bull that had never been lassoed.

But for all her intelligence, Jessie had sure developed a blind spot for Lord Clinton Bly. He was a scoundrel of the worst order. A man as dangerous as any in the world, Shaw thought. In fact, Shaw wondered if Bly had ever been associated with the cartel. Or was he trying to fill the void left by its demise?

Passing under the carriage portico, Shaw strode up the steps and across the hotel lobby. Lost in his thoughts of

Jessie and her blindness to Lord Clinton Bly, Shaw had almost reached the steps before he realized the desk clerk was calling him.

"Mr. Shaw, Mr. Shaw," the red-haired clerk shouted. "Message for you." He waved a yellow envelope over his head.

Shaw spun around and headed for the desk, almost running into an elderly couple that had been headed for the stairs. Shaw knew the telegram would be an important one, either from New Orleans or from the capital, with information on the gun shipment that had left New Orleans.

At the desk, the clerk gave Shaw the telegram. Despite his impulses to rip open the message, Shaw tucked it in his pocket and started back toward the stairs. It was better to take his time so no observer might assign undue importance to the message. At the top of the stairs, he pulled the key to Jessie's room from his pants pocket and let himself in. He could hear her singing softly in the bathroom as he locked the door behind him, then pulled the envelope from his pocket and tore it open. He saw that it was from headquarters, then read the message aloud. "Shipment Galveston bound. Arrive tonight."

He had been right. Lord Clinton Bly had to be involved. This was no mere coincidence. Tonight, he knew he had to investigate. If he could confirm the connection to Bly, he could prevent trouble along the border and save untold lives. He could arrest the Englishman and end the industrialist's evil plans.

Shaw toyed with telling Jessie, but discarded the idea. She had been taken in by Bly and would not believe his accusations. Better to get proof first, then lay it out before her. She was a reasonable woman and would believe facts.

He heard her emerge from the bathroom, and turned to see her pass by the door, a towel wrapped around her hair and her body. He hid the telegram behind his back, then stuffed it in his pocket when she disappeared from view. He cleared his throat as he moved into the bedroom. She was as desirable as before, but now he had to devote his complete attention to how he could protect her and still find out what he needed about the gun shipment. He had to know what Jessie's evening plans were.

Jessie tried to pretend he wasn't around, but Shaw caught an occasional glimpse of her eyes casting furtive glances at him.

"I'll buy you dinner tonight," Shaw said.

Jessie ignored him.

"I'll buy you dinner," he repeated.

Jessie turned around with a hairbrush and pulled the towel turban from her head. "I've other plans."

"What?"

"After how you followed us all day and humiliated me in front of Clinton Bly, you think I'll tell you?"

Shaw shrugged. "I can follow you like I did before. Or I can always arrest you. After all, the governor said to protect you. The Scorpion, remember?"

"This Scorpion business is bound to be a fairy tale."

"What are your plans, Jessie?"

"We are dining with Bly on his yacht. And you are not invited."

Though Shaw wasn't enamored with leaving Jessie on the yacht alone with Bly, he knew it would give him time to check out the railroad freight yards and the docks themselves. "Will Ki be with you?"

Jessie nodded. "He always is." Now Jessie stood with her hands on her hips. "I am tired of your embarrassing us. Lord Clinton Bly is not as bad as his reputation and we've business to discuss tonight."

"Tonight you will see how bad Lord Clinton Bly is," Shaw said, figuring he would have the goods on the Englishman by midnight. "My job is to watch out for you. I will follow you to the dock, see you on board the ship, then stay out of sight until you leave. Then I'll follow you back. I believe you are in danger, Jessie."

"From Bly?"

"Possibly."

"From The Scorpion?" Jessie asked, her tone full of skepticism.

"Maybe more so. Bly is a known quantity. The Scorpion is not."

Jessie laughed. "Maybe Bly is The Scorpion, if he exists at all."

Shaw nodded with no sign of a grin. "Perhaps."

"Stop your insults." Jessie threw her hairbrush at him.

Shaw's hand snapped the brush from the air. "What time are you leaving for the yacht?"

"Why should I tell you?"

"Because I'll pester you or get a search warrant and board Bly's ship, saying you were abducted."

"You'd do it too. Bly said he would send Mai Lay to our rooms to get us about eight o'clock."

Walking within reach of Shaw, Jessie cast her towel aside and moved to the closet, where she pulled out another dress she had had sent to her room for her stay. She casually began to dress. Shaw knew she was tempting him so she would have the pleasure of refusing his advances. He gritted his teeth and endured this pleasant torture.

Unable to take any more temptation, Shaw walked past her, tossed her hairbrush on the bed, and stepped outside on the balcony. The air wore a chill, and a long, low bank of gray clouds was moving in from the Gulf. The sun's light was a dying glow on the western horizon, and the air seemed to drip with moisture. To cut the chill, Shaw walked around the balcony, passing the door to Jessie's suite and then the door to Ki's. He saw Ki glance up from the floor where he was seated with legs crossed. The *ninja* seemed perturbed by Shaw's presence, then appeared to ignore the disturbance and slip into some deep trance.

Shaw looked toward the Gulf again, and realized the approaching cloud bank was actually fog beginning to roll in. At first, Shaw dreaded the chill and the fog because it would make it more difficult to keep up with Jessie when he followed her. And yet, it would provide him the cover he needed to explore the docks by Bly's yacht.

For a half hour, Shaw paced the balcony, killing time. Then, a few minutes before eight, he entered Jessie's bedroom again. "The air's turned nippy, Jessie. Do you have a wrap?"

Jessie looked at him, then pursed her lips. "Why do you have to be so stubborn? This would be so much easier if you weren't."

"You wouldn't like me any other way and I can't change."

Jessie moved to her closet and took a shawl from inside. It didn't complement her dark blue dress, but she apparently had no other wraps to choose from.

"It doesn't match, but I didn't expect it to turn cool."

"You look good in anything, Jessie."

She smiled, but before she thanked him for the compliment, a soft rap came from the door. She picked up her room key from the bed and nodded to Shaw. "Please don't embarrass me tonight."

Shaw followed her to the door and opened it. Mai Lay stood before them, wearing a formal kimono, though her face was not so heavily powdered tonight. She stood with her arms clasped in front of her, her hands hidden by the flowing sleeves of the silk dress.

"Please, I take you now," she said very formally.

"Good evening, Mai Lay," said Jessie.

Shaw nodded and lifted his key to lock the door, but Mai Lay reached for the key and, with a firm grip, snatched it from between his fingers. Mai Lay had a powerful grip, Shaw thought.

"I shall lock for you. Lord Bly says treat you as I treat him." She stepped to the door, but the key slipped from her hands onto the floor. She bent by the door, the key momentarily hidden by the folds of her dress as she ran her hand along the doorsill for it. Finding it, she picked it up, rose, and locked the door.

Shaw took the key from her and let it slide into his pocket as he followed the two women to Ki's room. Mai Lay rapped softly on his door, and Ki emerged quickly and locked his door.

The four walked down the stairs and outside. The air was thick with fog as they approached the rented buggy Mai Lay had driven back to the hotel. Beside the buggy, Mai Lay turned to Shaw. "Do not think me rude," she said, "but Lord Bly said you were not invited, please."

"I just came down to help Miss Starbuck aboard," he said. He turned to Jessie and whispered, "Be careful."

Jessie nodded as he assisted her into the buggy. Saying nothing more, he walked away from the Crown Hotel, taking the route he figured the buggy would follow to the yacht. Shortly, the buggy passed him and he caught a glimpse of Jessie staring at him in the fog. He trotted behind the buggy, just keeping it in sight. He wanted to make sure Jessie and Ki made it safely aboard Bly's yacht before he began his own explorations.

When he finally caught the sinister shape of Bly's yacht in the fog, he was in time to see Jessie, Ki, and Mai Lay get out of the buggy and walk down the pier and up the gangplank. He watched them disappear into the ship near the bridge, then advanced down the dock, hiding behind the crates and freight stacked there. Toward the end of the dock, he heard the noise of men at work. He slipped in that direction, studying the ship. Originally a freighter, it had been converted into a yacht. Or had it? Shaw wondered. Finally he could see men rolling crates up a gangplank and depositing them in a cargo hold. One by one crates from a stack the size of a house were being loaded onto the ship.

Shaw slipped past a couple guards with rifles and got close enough to read the crates. They were labeled "DYNAMITE." Shaw caught his breath. He had expected rifles and small arms and ammunition, but not this. Bly was equipping a small army, and the rifles would arrive later tonight. He had been right about Bly. There was no need now to go to the railroad yards.

Now, would Jessie believe him? He avoided the guards,

117

retreated back down the pier, and took up a position in an alley across the street to wait out Ki and Jessie, then make sure they got back safely to the Crown Hotel.

After a meal of fresh lobster with lemon sauce, Lord Clinton Bly waved his hand at the cabin boy. "We shall have dessert later. Please leave and see that we are not disturbed until I ring."

"Yes, sir," replied the waiter as he stepped backward from the dining room and closed the metal door.

The dining room was cozy but more luxurious than Jessie would have imagined for an iron paddle steamer like Bly's yacht. The dining table of highly polished mahogany reflected the solid gold chandelier that hung overhead. Though the dining table could accommodate six, it was set for four, with Jessie and Bly at opposite ends and Ki and Mai Lay seated across from each other.

Jessie knew why Bly was delaying dessert. He wanted to discuss business. Though she had found him a more complex man than she had originally anticipated, she doubted she wanted to do business with him. It seemed odd to her that a man with his business skills would offer to pay more than the market price for cotton.

Bly cleared his throat, propped his elbows on the table, and held his hands fingertip to fingertip. Jessie felt his hard gaze upon her. "Now, good lady, we must discuss business. Much as I have enjoyed your acquaintance these past two days, I must be entirely candid with you. When I do business with people, I like to know them, get a feel for their strengths and their weaknesses. You are like your father, a person of ironclad integrity."

Jessie felt herself soften at the mention of her father's name. Bly was shrewd to invoke the hallowed name of Alex Starbuck because it had an effect upon her. "Father was a good man."

"Indeed he was, good lady," Bly replied. "You are like him. Your strength is your only weakness."

118

"A strength," countered Jessie, "is never a weakness."

"You speak of character, but I speak of business. No, good lady, they are different, but we digress from the main issue. I want to buy your cotton. All of it."

Here it comes, Jessie thought, trying to figure the angle. "The cotton's for sale on the open market. Nothing's to keep you from buying all you want."

"Perhaps not, but why buy in small lots at different times when I can buy your entire supply at once? I am prepared to offer you a price ten percent . . . no, for you, fifteen percent above the going rate for all the cotton coming out of Texas after the fall harvest."

"What do you want in return for your generosity?"

"A five-year contract to buy all your cotton."

Jessie crossed her arms across her chest. "At fifteen percent above market prices?"

Lord Bly licked his lips. "That would be foolish, as you know. The final four years of the contract would be at the market price."

Now it made sense. Her cotton export manager, Martin Bark, had been right in his assessment of Bly's motives. And Wade Shaw had been right as well. "Have you made this offer to other exporters in the country or just me?" she asked, knowing that he would be lying if he denied it.

"Indeed not, good lady, you're the only one."

Jessie smiled. "My information says you have offered similar deals with other cotton exporters throughout the South."

Bly shook his head, pulled his hands apart, and pointed his index finger at Jessie. "Lest you think you've caught me in an untruth, I must admit I have dealt with others. But I have offered not one of them a similar deal. They do not have your strength of integrity, and will sell for much less than the fifteen percent I am offering you."

Now Jessie shook her head. "As I see it, I've gained very little if you pay me fifteen percent above market price for the first year of a five-year contract, then the market price for the remaining four years, especially if you control the market."

"You'll have averaged a three-percent gain above market price over the course of the contract."

"If you're contracted for all the cotton, you'll control the market. You'll in effect set the market price, and all the families in Texas that are sweating to make a good crop and make a decent living will be hurt by such market manipulations. Only you will profit. You'll buy low and sell high to the textile mills."

Bly smiled and cocked his head. "You're a shrewd one, good lady, but your strength is your weakness. You've too much integrity to hold your own in this age of industrial progress. Your fashion of business is going the way of the sailing ship."

"Fair dealing never goes out of style. You disappoint me."

"And you, good lady, disappoint me, but I shall give you time to think. I leave day after tomorrow and you have until then to give me your answer."

"I can give you my answer now," Jessie said, standing up and throwing her napkin on the bone china plate before her. "No!"

"You should reconsider, good lady," Bly said, his eyes narrowing and his jaw jutting forward, "or you will find the Starbuck empire will be devoured by Bly Industries. At present, I am only a threat to your cotton business. If you spurn my offer, I am a threat to your entire empire, good lady."

Jessie turned to Ki. "It is time we left." Ki seemed disturbed by this turn of events, his questioning gaze lingering on Mai Lay.

Bly stood up, took the handbell by his side, and shook it. Instantly, the cabin boy reappeared. "Please bring the lady's wrap," Bly instructed, before turning to Jessie. "I'm most apologetic that we could not find a way to a satisfactory deal, good lady, though you still have time to reconsider."

"All the time in the world will not change my mind, Lord

Bly," Jessie said as she took her shawl from the cabin boy.

"You have until day after tomorrow to reconsider," he said, then turned to Mai Lay. "Please return Miss Starbuck and Mr. Ki to the hotel and then handle the other chores I've assigned you."

Mai Lay bowed to Bly. "As you wish."

★

Chapter 14

Ki waited for Jessie to pass before walking out of the dining room behind her and Mai Lay, who led them past the bridge toward the gangplank. As they marched out on the deck, sailors stopped loading cargo as they passed the hold, and Ki had the distinct impression the crew was trying to hide something from them. As Ki walked from amidships to the stern and the gangplank nearest the shore, he glanced back over his shoulder to see exactly what was going on. The sailors just stared back.

As Ki neared the rear gangplank, a half-dozen crew members were coming aboard, each carrying a rifle. A couple of sailors jerked their caps down low over their faces, and another jumped toward a ventilator cowl and hid behind it. Something about the one behind the ventilator cowl seemed familiar to Ki, but he just couldn't place him. He took a step in that direction, planning to see for himself, then felt Mai Lay's surprisingly strong grip upon his arm.

"Please," she said, "go we must."

Ki stood a moment longer, staring at the cowl.

"Please," Mai Lay repeated.

Ki acquiesced and started down the gangplank, Mai Lay bringing up the rear. As they stepped on the dock, Ki paused to look to the far end of the pier. In the murkiness, he thought he saw the shape of another man carrying a rifle, as if he were on guard, but Mai Lay hurried him along toward the rented buggy. In front of him, Jessie shivered in her shawl, but Mai Lay seemed comfortable, even in the thin silk kimono she was wearing.

At the end of the dock, they passed a dinghy tied to a piling. Ki noted the dinghy, thinking about returning in the night and rowing around Bly's yacht to see what was really going on. He wondered if that was his real motive, or if he just wanted another chance to see Mai Lay. They had been together much the last two days, but never alone. Ki felt his desire for her building, and he wondered if he could ever have her. The rift between Jessie and Lord Clinton Bly, even though he agreed with Jessie's stand, jeopardized his chances with Mai Lay.

Reaching the buggy, he helped Jessie onto the seat beneath the canopy, then escorted Mai Lay around the back of the rig. He stopped by the rear wheel and grabbed Mai Lay, pulling her to him. She came willingly and he bent his neck to kiss her. She pressed her lips to his and seemed to mold her body against his. He rubbed his hand over her back and understood why she was not cold. Beneath her thin silk kimono she wore another garment, what felt like a twill-cotton blouse. He let his hand slide down to her buttocks and realized she was wearing soft cotton pants as well. Then he pulled his lips from her and held her back with one hand as he cupped her breast with the other. She caught her breath and seemed to shove her breast against his palm. Ki's desire hardened.

"Tonight," she said. "We must tonight."

Ki lowered his head and kissed her again, then broke away at the sound of Jessie's voice.

"You two okay?"

By the Jessie's tone, Ki knew she had an idea of what was going on. He didn't care. He just wanted Mai Lay. Then, across the street, he saw Wade Shaw watching through the fog's veil. Ki resented him for spying.

123

"Let's go," Ki said, guiding Mai Lay around the buggy, helping her onto the seat, then squeezing in beside her. Taking the reins, Ki started the buggy toward the Crown Hotel, snapping the leather strands against the horse. The animal lurched forward at a trot.

"Why the hurry, Ki?" asked Jessie.

"We're being followed."

"It is the one who always follows you," said Mai Lay.

"Yes." Ki nodded. "I want to teach him a lesson."

At the next corner where a few sailors were gathered, Ki stopped the buggy and jumped out. "You two go on."

"No," answered Jessie. "I don't want you hurting him, Ki. I'm staying." Before Ki could argue she jumped out of the buggy.

Ki tossed Mai Lay the reins. "Please, go on. Take the buggy to the stable. Wait there and I will escort you back to the yacht. Too many sailors out tonight for you to return by yourself."

"Yes," she replied, and Ki could sense the desire in her answer.

"Now go on," he said, slapping the horse on the rump. The horse and rig were soon lost in the fog, but the clip-clop of the shod hooves against the brick street carried through the fog.

"Ki," Jessie demanded, as a couple of sailors strolled up, "what do you plan to do to him?"

"Trip him and take his gun for pestering us so much."

Ki could hear the hard fall of boots hitting against the brick street as Wade Shaw ran toward them. He took Jessie's arm to pull her around the corner out of sight, but found the way blocked by two sailors. He moved to get around them and two more blocked his path. Then another pair closed a circle around them.

"I don't know what you plan to do with *him*," one said with a drunken sneer, "but we know what we plan to do with the lady."

Another shook his fist at Ki. "You're too damn ugly to have a woman like that all to yourself."

124

"Yeah," said another.

Before another word was said, Ki released Jessie. "Take her, boys."

The open invitation caught the sailors unprepared, and in that moment of hesitation Ki unleashed a furious barrage. Like a catapult, he loosed his foot into the groin of the first sailor who had spoken.

Instantly, the sailor spoke eloquently of pain with a scream that bounced through the fog.

With a chop to the neck from the side of his steel-rimmed hand, Ki downed another one, who groaned on the walk.

From opposite sides, two men charged, planning to squeeze him between them, but Ki ducked, rolled out of the way, and bounced to his feet just as they clasped each other in a surprised hug.

Spinning around, Ki lunged for them, grabbing them by their long hair and jerking their heads apart. They screamed only for the instant it took him to slam their heads together. With a sickening thud, the pair stopped their complaints as their wobbly knees gave way and they fell to the ground.

With a reverse kick, Ki hit the fifth sailor in the gut, momentarily winding him. As the last sailor rushed him, Ki leaped into the air and loosed a frightful kick that landed full force in the man's nose, and he tumbled to the ground, his face a bloody mess.

The sailor still on his feet was doubled over holding his stomach, trying to get his breath. Ki clasped his hands together and raised them like a club over the gasping man's head. Then he lowered the boom, and the final sailor fell to the ground.

As Ki caught his breath, he heard Jessie behind him. "Well, done, Ki."

"I agree," said Wade Shaw.

Ki scowled at the Ranger. "Let's get to the hotel."

"Why'd you leave the wagon?" Shaw asked as they started toward the hotel.

"We were being followed," Ki said, "and I wanted to teach him a lesson."

125

"It was me," Shaw answered.

"I know," Ki replied, and saw the look of shock on the Ranger's face.

Jessie interrupted. "You were right about Bly."

"And there's some things I've got to tell you about him," Shaw said. "But we need to wait until we're in your room and sure no one is eavesdropping."

Ki saw Wade Shaw slip his arm around Jessie, and it reminded him how much he wanted Mai Lay. He stepped around the downed sailors and started for the hotel. He could hear Jessie and Shaw following behind him.

At the side street beside the Crown Hotel he waited for Jessie and Shaw, then fell in beside them as far as the hotel stable. "I must escort Mai Lay back to the yacht. I may not see her again."

"I am sorry, Ki," said Jessie. She reached out and patted his shoulder. "I'll be okay with Wade."

Ki nodded as he turned down the alley and walked to the door that was ajar. The stable was dark and Ki could just make out the back of the buggy a few feet inside as he entered. "Mai Lay?" he called softly. Only the blowing and stamping of the stabled horses answered him. "Mai Lay?" he called again. A soft moan answered him. "Are you okay?" he asked, stepping toward the noise.

He moved deeper into the darkness. Then he heard a swish of straw near him. He turned to see if Mai Lay approached.

Suddenly, his head exploded with a thousand burning streaks of light that bounced around inside his brain. He started falling, and then all was a dull throbbing darkness without time and memory.

Jessie drew closer to Wade Shaw, and she relished his arm around her. Shaw was a good man and his suspicions were true. Jessie felt she had been taken in by Lord Clinton Bly, who was good at assessing weaknesses. He understood her weakness was her father. By speaking highly of him, Bly knew he would win her initial trust. Shaw was as open as a

126

book. He didn't play those games. He spoke his feelings and if he was wrong, he admitted it. Jessie liked that in a man.

They turned the corner toward the front of the hotel. She could just make out the shape of the carriage portico in the fog. The night's unseasonable chill had driven decent folks inside and not a person waited outside. Wade's powerful arm around her shoulder felt comforting, and she warmed to his touch in spite of the chill.

She had so many things to say to him that she could hardly contain herself as they walked up the steps and inside the hotel. She was enveloped by the building's warmth as they marched toward the stairs. Quickly they were up the stairs and standing outside the door. As Shaw fumbled for the key in his pocket, Jessie turned to kiss him full on the lips. His body felt so natural against hers.

He broke himself away from her lips. "Not so fast, Jessie. We've got things to talk about."

"I was wrong," Jessie began as he opened the door. "We can talk about the rest of it later."

Wade managed to insert the key in the lock, then open the door. He motioned for Jessie to go in. She stood just inside the door as he stepped past her to light a gas lamp.

As Wade adjusted the lamp, the dimness receded in the corner and Jessie closed the door. As she moved to lock it, her shoe slipped on something on the floor.

Stepping back, she saw a piece of paper. Shaw saw it too as she bent to pick it up. Jessie grabbed a corner, then lifted the paper. It took but a moment's glance for a chill as cold as ice to race up her spine.

Shaw snatched the paper from her fingers and stared at it. Jessie saw his eyes narrow. On the paper before him was the ink representation of a scorpion.

"The Scorpion has found you, Jessie," Shaw said, his eyes filled with worry. "Now do you believe me?"

Jessie nodded. "Who could it be?"

Shaw stepped past her and slipped his key into the lock to secure the door. "I figure it's Bly."

"He was with us for dinner."

"He could have had one of his men do it. Whatever you do, Jessie, don't visit him again, especially on the yacht."

Shaw heard footsteps by the door, and motioned for Jessie to move back into the bedroom. He pulled his gun and waited, but the footsteps trailed off down the hallway.

Jessie let out a deep breath.

"Maybe we better move into the bedroom," he said as he let his gun slide back in his holster. He lit another gas lamp and looked about the room.

Jessie moved over and carefully opened up the closet to check inside. It was empty. Wade examined the bathroom without finding anything amiss.

"We've got to watch your every move now, Jessie."

She nodded and felt suddenly chilled. The door to the balcony was slightly ajar. Had she forgotten to close it when she left? She moved that direction.

"Where you going?" Wade asked. "You need to stay away from the windows." Shaw stepped to intersect her path.

"You worry too much," Jessie said.

No sooner had she spoke than the door swung open, as if pulled by sinister forces.

For a flash of an instant, her brain registered a dark-clad figure against the fuzzy gray of the fog. She caught the glint of a blade being raised, and then she felt herself knocked down.

Jessie hit the floor hard and rolled out from under Shaw. The Texas Ranger scrambled to his feet and jerked his .45-caliber revolver free. He squeezed off a shot through the open door and scared the knife-throwing attacker away. Jessie jumped to her feet and glanced from the now-vacant door to Shaw. He looked from the window to where a stiletto had sprouted from his shoulder. Jerking the knife out, he dropped it on the floor and ran out onto the balcony, Jessie upon his heels.

They saw a black ghost leap over the balcony. They ran to the railing in time to see the figure land nimbly, then run down the street. Shaw fired once, then again as the figure turned around the corner.

"Dammit," he said, bolting past Jessie, through the bedroom, and toward the door.

"Wait, Wade, you're hurt," Jessie cried.

"You stay here and don't leave," he commanded, shoving his gun in its holster and digging out the key from his pocket. He quickly unlocked the door, stuck his key in his pocket, and ran out into the hall, looking both ways for potential ambushers.

"Take your key and keep the door locked until I get back," he commanded as he ran down the hallway for the stairs.

Jessie grabbed her key and quickly locked the door. She ran to the balcony in time to see Wade Shaw, pistol in hand, run out of the hotel. He turned in the direction the assailant had taken.

"Be careful," Jessie called, "be careful."

As he faded in the fog, Jessie retreated inside, locking the balcony door behind her. She picked up the knife with Shaw's blood upon it and threw it against the wall in anger.

She walked over to her bed and slid her hand beneath the mattress, pulling out her pistol from where she had hidden it. The gun was a Colt .38-caliber revolver mounted on a .44 frame. She would take nothing for granted again in Galveston and she would go nowhere without the revolver.

She wished Ki hadn't stayed behind to see Mai Lay back to the yacht. Now all Jessie could do was wait. It was a long wait, and she never heard Ki return. Eventually she turned out the gas lamp in the bedroom, leaving the one lit in the drawing room for Wade Shaw when he returned. When he came back, she would summon a doctor to tend his wound and she would tend his other needs. Tired from digging for Lafitte's treasure, Jessie could not wait any longer. She fell asleep.

★

Chapter 15

Slowly his senses returned to him. First, he felt the pounding in his head, the banging against the inside of his skull. Then the throbbing ache pulsated throughout his head, down his neck, and into his shoulders. Next he caught the stiff aroma of hay mixed with manure, then realized he was sprawled on the stable floor. At first, Ki could not remember what he was doing in the stable. Then he thought of Mai Lay and his intent to escort her back to the yacht.

Where was she? What had happened?

Pushing himself to his hands and knees, he lingered on the stable floor, trying to collect his wits. He shook his head to clear the muddle in his mind, but only succeeded in making his head throb worse than before.

Ki turned toward the stable door, grimacing as he crawled for the opening. He had to struggle to move hand, knee, hand and knee across the straw-carpeted floor. As he neared the corner of the door, his lead hand fell upon a rag. His fingers wrapped around it and he lifted it to his face, wiping away the straw and grime that had stuck there. Gingerly, he brushed the rag against the knot on the back of his head, and winced at the slightest touch. He started to toss the rag aside, but his muddled brain realized this was no ordinary stable rag. It was too soft and cool. It had the feel of silk.

For a moment he couldn't make sense of it, but then he held it up to his nose. The material had the aroma of a woman. Not just any woman, but Mai Lay! Ki panicked. He remembered the sailors who had tried to attack Jessie. Had Mai Lay been attacked? Where was she? Was she safe? His throbbing head seemed aflutter with questions for which he had no answers. He had to find her. He pushed himself to his feet, stumbling toward the door and grabbing hold of it. The still-unharnessed buggy horse stamped his feet and tossed his head nervously. Ki steadied himself, giving his head a chance to clear. He lost track of time, but stood there several minutes until his balance steadied. Then he stepped through the doorway into the alley.

The cool, moist air felt good against his skin, and helped revive him enough that he could start down the street toward the docks and toward Lord Clinton Bly's yacht. Except for a drunken sailor sitting in a stupor on the walk, the street was now empty of all but the fog and the coolness. He moved unsteadily but with determination along the docks. As he neared the Bly yacht, he heard the sounds of men loading freight. Though it struck him as odd they would be working this late and in the dark, he lacked the strength to investigate.

Finally reaching the dock where the Bly yacht was moored, he saw an armed sailor standing guard. The slicker-clad seaman wore a cap at a tilt on his head. Ki did not notice the patch covering one of the sailor's eyes.

"State your business!" the guard growled.

Ki stopped and looked at the man. There was something vaguely familiar about him, but Ki couldn't make the connection with anything that seemed very important now.

"I've got to find her." Ki felt unsteady on his feet for a moment.

"Who, your mother?" The sailor laughed. "You drunk, mate?"

"Mai Lay," Ki said.

"The Chink girl? She's fine, mate."

"I've gotta see." Ki advanced a step.

The sailor shoved his rifle against Ki's chest. "Go on, Chink boy, before you get hurt."

"I've gotta see her." Ki repeated. When he was thinking straight, he knew he could disarm this sailor in an instant, but now he knew better than to try.

"What's the problem?" said a voice from down the dock.

"A Chink boy wants to see Mai Lay," the sailor answered.

The unseen voice came back. "I'll send the word for her to appear on deck. We don't want any more trouble tonight."

Ki could make out the noise of an order being shouted from mouth to mouth down the dock and up the yacht. He walked away from the guard to the edge of the pier and stared at the dinghy tethered to the piling. Shortly, he heard Mai Lay's voice.

"Ki? I'm okay, Ki."

He saw her standing at the railing at the yacht's stern.

"I found your kimono," he said.

"Some men attacked me, the same ones that knocked you out," she explained. "They ripped it from me, but I got away when the Texas Ranger ran by chasing some man. Are you okay?"

Ki nodded. "As long as you are safe, I'm okay."

"Then go to your room, Ki, and farewell. I've been ordered by Lord Bly not to see you again and I must do what he says."

Ki sighed. There was nothing more he could say. "Bye," he said, and turned around for the hotel. The anticipation of finding Mai Lay safe was replaced by the disappointment that he would not see her again.

Glancing over his shoulder, he saw Mai Lay running along the deck, then disappearing in the fog. Ki stepped off the dock and angled across the street. He had barely gone a block when a terrible scream pierced the air. It was a horrifying scream that was lost in a sudden inexplicable blast of the yacht's steam whistle.

132

Ki flinched at the shrill whistle, then stumbled back to the hotel, not knowing how long it took, nor caring. He vaguely remembered Mai Lay mentioning the Texas Ranger, but it did not register. After all, Wade Shaw was protecting Jessie tonight.

Finally, Ki made it to the hotel and pushed his way inside. He could feel the desk clerk staring at him and his dirty, smelly clothes. Ki just shook his head and kept moving across the lobby to the stairs. Each step seemed to get higher than the last one, and he was exhausted by the time he reached the top of the stairs. He turned down the hallway and stumbled toward his room. He managed to unlock his door, then trudged to his bed.

He pulled his clothes off and let them fall on the floor, then lunged naked for the mattress. Collapsing on the covers, he realized he should have turned them first. He struggled to pull them back with himself atop them and finally managed to succeed. With that he crawled between the sheets. The mattress was like heaven to his aching body and he fell into a deep, soothing sleep that shut out the rest of the world. He drifted into such a deep sleep that he might have slept for hours had he not felt the covers being slowly pulled back from his chest. The movement was so slight, so patient, that at first he thought he was dreaming. And then he felt a soft hand upon his manhood.

Ki opened his eyes slightly and took in the dark shape of a woman. She tickled his groin with her fingers, but said nothing. As his eyes gradually adjusted to the dim light thrown off by the glow of the fog, Ki smiled. It was Mai Lay.

"You came," he said.

"I slipped away after Lord Bly went to sleep," she explained. "I might not have another chance to be with you."

"But all the guards."

"They are easy to outsmart," she said, "but you talk too much. I have come to ease your aches. Be silent and enjoy what I offer."

133

Ki smiled again, and turned to watch as Mai Lay removed her hand from his groin and stepped back into a block of light pudding in from the window. She stepped out of her kimono and let it slide to the floor. In spite of the pain from the knot on his head, Ki twisted on his pillow to watch. She had a svelte body that was medicine to Ki's eyes if not the bump on his head. "You're beautiful," he offered.

"You're talking again," she replied. "You must stop."

She lifted her hands to her head, her firm breasts rising as well while she pulled out three stiletto-like hairpins. Her hair tumbled from her head, dropping all the way past her waist.

Until now, Ki had only seen her hair in a bun. He liked it better this way. Mai Lay ran her fingers through the long strands of black hair, guiding a handful over her shoulder and letting it fall over her left breast. She draped a second handful of hair over her right breast as well. Ki focused on her dark nipples as they peeked through her long hair.

Mai Lay advanced toward him. She knew the ways of her ancestors, and Ki knew that also meant the ways of physical fulfillment. She moved slowly like a lioness on the prowl. As she came close to the bed, his eyes fell naturally to that black butterfly at the vee of her legs. The hair there was petitely trimmed and inviting. Ki nodded, despite the throb from the knot on his head. She knew how to groom herself for lovemaking.

Just above the trim of her bush, Ki just made out a small mole or scar, but could not be certain which it was. He reached out to touch her there, but Mai Lay took his hand.

"I do all the work," she said.

She placed his hand back upon the bed, then bent over and began to caress her fingers lightly over his face.

Ki tingled to her touch and twisted slightly on the pillow, moaning equally from the pleasure of her touch and the ache from the knot on his head.

Mai Lay came closer until he could feel her warm breath upon his face. With her lips, she began to trail her fingers across his face, gently at first, then harder as her lips crossed his.

Unable to take any more, Ki reached up with his hand and pulled her lips tightly against his, then groaned at the spasm of pain his sudden movement caused.

"See," Mai Lay chided, "you must be still. I must treat you."

When he resisted, Mai Lay pulled away. Ki sighed, then submitted to her wishes, letting his hand drop from her.

Once again she started to caress his face, then bathe it with gentle, moist kisses. When her mouth came across his again, she parted her lips and nibbled at his, once playfully biting at his upper lip.

As she kissed, she began to let her tongue slide into his mouth, darting teasingly in and out. Her hands roamed from his cheeks, down his jaw, past his neck to his chest, where they slid gently up and down. Wherever her hands went, her mouth and tongue soon followed. She broke from his lips and trailed kisses down Ki's chin to his neck, then his shoulder, and finally his chest, paying particular attention to his nipples.

Ki thrilled to her touch. He had wanted her so badly, and soon he would have her. His desire was hardening more than he thought possible, and his hips began to rise impatiently for relief.

Mai Lay lifted her lips from his nipple. "Patience is a virtue that makes anticipation all the better," she said.

Ki's hips dropped back to the bed, and were stilled while Mai Lay waited to resume her playful torture. Ki knew that the agony of anticipation would only make passion's final explosion more intense, but it was becoming harder and harder to withstand the pleasure.

Mai Lay straddled Ki at the waist and began to massage his chest, then began to ease her hips toward his throbbing manhood. For a brief instant, Ki felt himself at the entry to her trimmed little box of Asian delights, but Mai Lay slid her hips on past his waist and down to his knees.

135

Ki groaned in disappointment.

"Patience," she replied.

Her fingers skated lightly down his hard stomach to his waist, lingering just an eyelash away from his pulsing desire, then retreating back to his stomach and circling his navel.

Once more Ki groaned in disappointment, but that seemed to be the cue Mai Lay was awaiting. Her hands rushed to his manhood, surrounding it softly with one hand while she used the index finger of her other hand to circle the tip of his passion prod.

Ki moaned now, the pleasure so intense that it overpowered his headache.

With her soft, gentle hands she then kneaded his flesh, and then when Ki thought he could take no more, she leaned forward and took him full in the mouth, then retreated to the very tip of his manhood and circled it with quick laps of her tongue.

She was a master of the sensual arts, never moving so fast that Ki's lust would explode, but always keeping him on the verge. Ki lost track of time and everything except Mai Lay. She was so much more than he had expected.

Finally, she pulled her lips away from him and began to slide her body back up his until her legs neared his waist. This time she was an open invitation, and Ki directed himself into the moist folds at the base of her petitely trimmed bush. He began to lift his hips and press his desire into the warmth between her legs, but she sat down hard upon him, pinning his hips against the bed.

"I must do it," she said.

Ki moaned in expectant frustration.

"You will like it better if I do it," she said.

Ki gritted his teeth and tried to allow all his muscles—save one—to relax.

"That's better," Mai Lay said as she straddled him on her knees. She began to raise her hips a couple times and settle onto Ki's manliness. Then she stopped.

Ki looked at her and let his hands begin to explore her

body, running first up her muscled thighs, then over her tight stomach, and finally to her firm breasts. Instead of the softness he was accustomed to in women, Mai Lay possessed a lean, muscled body that made her all the more exciting to him. Ki squeezed her firm breasts in his hands, thumbing at her nipples.

"I am ready. Are you?" Mai Lay whispered.

"I've been ready."

Mai Lay smiled. "I know, but this will be better." She began the final assault upon his manhood, but instead of lifting herself up and down on her knees, she began to stroke him without raising up. The muscles within her seemed to grasp and tug at him as she flexed and relaxed her powerful stomach muscles.

"Oh, that is so good," he cried out in spite of himself.

And Mai Lay just continued contracting and relaxing around his manhood, as if her insides were trying to pull all of him within her. He had never felt himself so aroused, and his entire groin tingled with the slow anticipation of relief. It seemed as if she were stretching him even more within her.

For ten, fifteen, twenty minutes she continued to stoke him while sitting perfectly still upon his hips. Then the fire of desire that had been burning within him seemed to spread to Mai Lay. She began to moan, and she closed her eyes as she awaited his final burst of passion.

The muscles within her seemed to tug harder and faster around him until Ki gasped with pleasure. He felt his relief building deep within his body, slowly moving from within until his engulfed desire tingled, then exploded in a flood of passion. Ki squeezed her firm breasts and bucked his hips against hers.

Mai Lay screamed with ecstasy at Ki's release and her own, then collapsed on his chest, her breast against his, as he wrapped his strong arms around her.

For a few more minutes he brushed his hand through her hair as she nibbled at his chest. He wanted her to stay so he could return the favor, but shortly Mai Lay pushed herself away.

"It is but an hour until dawn," she said. "I must return before Lord Bly finds I am gone. He will be greatly displeased." She shook her head, her hair brushing against his chest. "We are bound to people. You to Miss Starbuck and me to Lord Bly. We cannot break those bonds, Ki, much though I wish we could."

Ki nodded as he continued to admire the silhouette of her body. "I could never leave Jessie, but at least she is honest."

Mai Lay began to wrap her long hair around her hands and pile it on her head before bending to pick up the stiletto hairpins. Once the hair was held by the pins, she answered Ki. "True, but Lord Bly did me many favors and I am indebted to do his bidding just as you are indebted to Miss Starbuck. Though Lord Bly has been mean to many others, he has always been decent with me."

For a moment, Ki sensed a tone of regret in her voice. "Has he commanded you to treat others as he treats them?"

Mai Lay ignored him as she pulled on her kimono.

"Answer my question," Ki demanded.

"Yes." She sighed.

"I can help you leave him," Ki offered. "Jessie'll help too."

"Had I not vowed otherwise, Ki, I would like that."

She moved toward the door, then stopped, almost too embarrassed to look back over her shoulder at him. "Perhaps I can see you tonight. It will be the last night before we leave for Mexico. Can we meet again?"

"Yes."

She turned around to face him. "It will be too risky for me to come here again. At the end of the docks, where the bay curves around, you will find a sandy beach and a place where only the wooden ribs of a sunken ship are half buried in the sand. Meet me there about ten."

"I will," Ki said.

Mai Lay left the room, and Ki stared at the door as it closed behind her. Already he looked forward to tonight, and even more, he regretted what it would mean. He would never see Mai Lay again.

He started to get up and lock the door behind her, but it was so close to dawn he didn't figure anybody would try to slip into the room so soon before light. He settled into bed and turned easily over on his side to lessen the pain from the bump on his head.

Gradually he drifted into sleep. His body was spent from the assault and the pleasure of Mai Lay's visit, so when he did doze off it was a deep sleep. He didn't sleep long, though, because it was barely dawn when the door to his room flew open with a bang.

Though he was lethargic, Ki lifted up from his pillow, the bump on his head sending spasms of pain all the way down into his neck. Ki tried to blink away the mud in his eyes and the muddle in his brain as he stared at the intruder.

He relaxed at the sound of Jessie calling his name, then recoiled at the terror of her words.

"Ki," she shouted, "something bad has happened. Wade Shaw has disappeared."

★

Chapter 16

Ki jumped from his bed, grimacing as his feet hit the carpeted floor and jarred loose the pain from the tender bump on his head. Jessie closed the door as Ki, trying to hide his nakedness, scrambled for the closet. He jerked on a pair of new jeans, grabbed a collarless shirt, and walked back out to Jessie, who had lit one of the gas lamps.

"Tell me what happened," Ki instructed as he slipped his arms into the twill cotton shirt and pulled it over his head. As the shirt brushed against the bump on his head, Ki grimaced.

Jessie saw his pain and rushed to his side, reaching to touch the knot.

Ki cursed in Japanese.

"What happened?" Jessie asked.

"I was knocked out in the stable. Now, what happened to Wade?"

"We were attacked in the room. I got just a glimpse of the man, small, dressed in black, nothing else I could see. Was it the same person?"

Carefully, Ki shook his head. "Mai Lay said she was attacked by sailors who ripped off her dress and tried to do more."

140

Still a bit woozy on his feet, Ki moved back over to the bed and sat down. As he did, Jessie moved over beside him and handed Ki a sheaf of paper.

Grabbing the paper, Ki began to unfold it. His mouth dropped when he saw the simple depiction of a scorpion with raised stinger. "Where'd this come from?"

"Last night," explained Jessie, "we found it under our door when Wade and I returned to the hotel."

"So The Scorpion is in Galveston."

"That's what Wade thinks." Jessie nodded and ran her fingers through her hair. "We moved into the bedroom to talk about Bly's offer to me and what Wade had found out. I felt a breeze from the balcony door and went to close it. When I did, the door flew open and I saw a black-shrouded figure standing there. Wade thought faster than me and tackled me. He took a knife in the shoulder that was meant for me.

"We both ran out onto the balcony in time to see the intruder drop to the street below. Wade fired off a couple shots, then ran out of the room and the hotel after the assassin, telling me to stay behind. It was so foggy, I knew I could never find Wade to help.

"I waited for him to return and finally fell asleep."

Ki cursed to himself. He should never have spent the night with Mai Lay because she had distracted him from his mission to guard Jessie. Maybe Wade Shaw was a good Texas Ranger, and Ki had to admit he was a good man, but Shaw was not a *ninja* like himself, not someone trained with a full repertoire of the martial arts.

Jessie looked at Ki. "Do you think The Scorpion is Lord Bly?"

Ki nodded.

"That might explain a lot of things," Jessie said.

Though Ki suspected Bly, he was still perplexed about a couple things. "Did you and Wade come right back to the hotel? No stops or anything?"

"After we left you at the stables, we weren't long getting up to the room."

Ki shook his head. "And you had just arrived home when the attack occurred?"

"Hadn't been there more than two, three minutes."

Refolding the drawing of the scorpion, Ki handed it to Jessie. "It would've been hard for Lord Bly to leave his yacht and arrive here about the same time we did without us remembering a horse or a wagon racing by."

"The note was left under the door while we dined with Lord Bly, but he could have had one of his men deliver it."

Ki touched the knot on his head. "And Wade hasn't been seen since?"

"That's right."

Arising gingerly from the bed, Ki looked at Jessie. "Was the door broken open or anything?"

"No."

"It's possible Bly could've saved a key from his stay before we arrived."

Jessie nodded.

"Either that or somebody entered from the balcony. It's possible, especially for someone with the proper training, to climb up a wall at the front of a building without being noticed. It was foggy last night, making it all the easier. Bly has the money to buy the best training in the world."

"We saw at dinner how ruthless Bly can be."

Ki got up easily from the bed, giving himself a moment to make sure his balance was okay. He started toward the balcony and heard Jessie trailing behind him.

"What do you need, Ki?"

"To look at the balcony."

Ki stared at the stone rail where it ran into the building past his door, and followed it all the way around to where it rejoined the building on the other side of Jessie's suite. "Here's what I'm after," he called.

Jessie scurried over to him.

Ki pulled a length of rope from over the edge of the railing. On the end was knotted a grappling hook that had latched over the rail when the would-be assassin climbed to the balcony. Ki coiled the rope and slid it over his shoulder. He pursed his lips and shook his head. He feared the worst for Wade Shaw. It angered Ki that he had not been around to protect both Jessie and the Ranger.

Jessie moved opposite Ki. "What are you thinking, Ki? About Wade Shaw?"

Ki looked away.

"What are you thinking, Ki?"

"I'm thinking we need to go to the city marshal's office and let folks there know that a Texas Ranger has disappeared."

Jessie spun around to avoid Ki's gaze. Ki pitied her because she felt about Wade Shaw the way he did about Mai Lay. "Let's finish getting dressed and report his disappearance," he said.

Jessie nodded halfheartedly and started for the hallway and her own room.

"Wait," Ki commanded. "Let me go with you."

Ki had her hold the rope and grappling hook while he pulled on socks and his ankle-high Wellington boots, then retrieved his freshly cleaned black leather vest covered with pockets and filled with *shuriken*. He slipped into the vest, then picked up his curve-bladed *tanto* from where he had left it on the floor last night in his rush to get into bed. He slipped the sheathed knife in the back waistband of his jeans.

Taking the rope back from Jessie, he pointed for the door. "Let's get your things," he said, "and be sure and wear your .38 revolver. We may need it before all is done."

Jessie went wordlessly out into the hall and stood at the door to her room as Ki locked his. Then Jessie opened her door without a key.

Ki chastised her. "Don't leave your room without locking it behind you." He moved in ahead of her and did a quick check of each room and the closet. "Everything's clear now."

As she walked by the dresser she deposited the paper with the scorpion on it. Still dressed in her evening attire, Jessie stepped to the closet and quickly changed into a riding outfit with riding skirt, silk blouse, and riding vest.

Jessie retrieved her garter holster from a dresser and slipped the derringer holder over her right leg. Then she picked up the .38-caliber revolver her father had had specially made for her on a .44 frame. She strapped the .38's belted holster around her waist.

"Are you ready?" Ki asked.

Jessie looked at the dresser a moment, then went over and picked up a sharp weapon, an oddly designed stiletto. "This is the knife that hit Wade instead of me."

Ki took it from her, studying it for a few seconds. It was unlike any stiletto he remembered seeing. It had an Oriental design, leading Ki to wonder if another *ninja* wise in the ways of combat, a man like himself, was behind the attack on Shaw and Jessie. After all, the rope and grappling hook were among the many weapons in a *ninja*'s arsenal. "We'll take this and show the marshal."

They exited the room together, and Ki waited as Jessie locked the door behind her. The hallway was dim in the early morning light as they reached the stairs and headed for the lobby. Quickly they were on the street and heading toward the city hall and the marshal's office. The air was still cool and moist, but the fog was beginning to thin. The streets were just coming alive as men began to go to their jobs on the docks, and a couple of kids were hawking the morning newspaper on street corners.

At the marshal's office, Ki tried to open the door, but it was locked. Through the barred windows, though, Ki could see a couple of men with badges on their chest playing cards on the desk. Ki knocked on the door again, and the two men looked over their shoulders.

One motioned for Ki to go away. "We open at eight," he yelled, then turned around and started dealing the next hand.

Ki began to beat on the door. He was still pounding on the entrance when it was suddenly jerked open.

"What the hell do you want, Chink?" the deputy yelled.

144

He was a slender man, narrow of eyes, girth, and mind. "Oh, sorry, ma'am," he said when he realized Jessie was with Ki. He stood ogling her for a moment.

"We're here," said Jessie, "to report a missing man. A Texas Ranger named Wade Shaw."

The deputy hiked the gunbelt up and called over his shoulder to his card-playing buddy. "Ernest, you heard of any Texas Ranger being in town?"

Ernest, much shorter and rounder but no brighter, shrugged. "Marshal didn't tell any of his deputies that I know about, Burton, and Rangers wouldn't come to town without notifying the marshal."

"Afraid we can't help you man since we don't know anything about any Rangers being here in the first place," Burton said.

Ki shook his head in disbelief. "Isn't it your job to find things out?"

Burton shrugged. "My job's to do what the marshal says, and the marshal ain't said I need to be looking for no Texas Rangers. Fact is, Texas Rangers are a bit arrogant. They don't think they can get into any trouble that they can't get out of. We're small potatoes in their minds and they're never around when you really need them."

"Like now," Ki replied sarcastically, "when you need a couple more card players."

Jessie stepped toward the deputy. "Last night we were attacked. . . ."

Ki grabbed her arm. "Come on, Jessie. These are small men with small minds. You can telegraph the governor and advise him."

Burton mocked them. "And when you're done, telegraph the president as well." The laughter of Ernest and Burton broke like jagged glass down the street until Burton slammed the door.

Grumbling to himself at the lawmen's ineptitude, Ki turned around and pulled Jessie by the arm. "We'll find him ourselves."

They retraced their way to the hotel. "Where was the last place you saw him, Jessie?"

"He turned down the side street, heading toward the bay."

At the Crown Hotel, Ki proceeded down the street and began to scour the walk and the road for clues.

"He didn't leave tracks, Ki," Jessie said.

"No, but you said he was wounded. He may have left blood." After a futile fifteen-minute search, Ki was about to give up when he spotted a small circle of red. "Here we are," he called to Jessie.

She ran to his side. "Could be anybody's blood."

"It's the only thing we've got to go on for sure, though we both know where it's going to lead."

They looked in the direction of Bly's yacht.

"Damn him," said Jessie. "If he hurt Wade, I'll see that he's punished if it takes my entire fortune to do it."

Ki nodded. "Maybe he'll be okay," he said without really believing it. Ki instructed Jessie to cross the street and check the opposite walk for blood. "He's bound to have crossed the street somewhere if his trail leads where I think it will."

Jessie began to patrol the far walk as Ki advanced toward the Crown Hotel stable. The odor of the stable brought back the memory of last night and how he had been slugged inside. He tried to remember all that had happened and all that Mai Lay had told him. He seemed to recall her saying she had been saved from the sailors who jumped her when the Texas Ranger ran past. How did she know it was the Texas Ranger? It was foggy.

His thoughts were interrupted by Jessie's cry. "Over here, Ki, over here."

Ki trotted across the street, the knot on his head still bothering him a bit. He joined Jessie, who squatted over the walk and pointed to a couple more spots of blood.

Together they advanced down the walk, the spots of blood becoming more frequent as they turned onto the street fronting the bay. The trail of blood led across the street and onto the wooden walk along the piers and docks.

146

Ki turned to Jessie. "I knew it."

Jessie grimaced. "Please let him be alive."

They strode along the walk, finally reaching the pier where Bly's yacht was moored. The trail of blood stopped at the foot of the pier. Ki pointed for Jessie to walk past the pier and circle out into the street to see if she could pick up the trail, while he advanced up the pier to board the yacht.

Ki had gone no more than a dozen paces when an armed sailor stepped out from behind a stack of crates.

"Say, mate, where the hell you think you're going?"

Ki stopped and studied the bearded fellow who stared at him with cocked head. Ki had seen this man somewhere before. It was the same sailor who had stopped him on the pier last night, but he had seen him somewhere before that.

The man twisted his head, and then Ki saw the eye patch. This was the man who had trailed him and Jessie out of the train station and the man who had been in on the robbery of Bly and Mai Lay. "No trespassing on this pier, unless you want me to bash your head in," the sailor growled.

For the moment, Ki opted to retreat. He would come back later in the day or night and explore the ship. He would find Wade Shaw, no matter what. He spun around and started for the street, his gaze falling from the dock to the dinghy tied to the first pier piling. That was when he saw the lump floating in the water. It was a body, floating face down, submerged from its feet to its waist, only its back and arms riding at the surface. Ki knew it was Wade Shaw.

He hoped not to alarm Jessie, but she seemed to realize something was amiss by either the length or the look of Ki's stare. She ran to the edge of the walk and peered into the water. When her eyes focused on the white floating lump, her hand flew instinctively to her face and she let out a little yelp of horror.

A passerby noticed the body and raised a cry. Others came running from across the street and other piers. A crowd of sailors had gathered on the back of Bly's yacht and along the pier, but not one made an effort to assist with the body.

Ki walked to the edge of the dock, untied the dinghy, and rowed out to the body. He steered the dinghy alongside, then shoved his hands under Shaw's water-bloated shoulders and struggled him aboard.

When Ki got him in the boat, he turned him over and recoiled in horror at what he saw. His chest was punctured with knife wounds, and on his belly was carved a scorpion.

★

Chapter 17

"Make way for the law," called a man who barged through the circle of spectators standing at the foot of the pier where Ki had placed Wade Shaw's body. Jessie had covered him with a tarp she had pulled from a freight wagon. The crowd parted as a clean-shaven man stepped to the middle of the circle. In his wake followed the two deputies Ki had encountered at the marshal's office earlier.

Though he knew the deputies would have been too late to save Wade Shaw, Ki felt a simmering anger toward them for their refusal to take his claim seriously. Ki wanted the legal matters to run their course quickly so he could find Mai Lay and confront her with questions about her role in all of this.

The marshal squatted down beside the tarp and lifted an edge far enough to see the body. Behind him, men craned their necks to get a glimpse of the body. As the marshal stood up, the skinny deputy who kept hoisting his gunbelt up to his waist pointed at Ki and Jessie.

"Them's the ones that did it," said Burton.

Ki stepped forward to confront him, but he felt Jessie grab his hand firmly.

The marshal stared hard at Jessie and Ki, then extended his hand. "I'm Jack Bayless, marshal of Galveston."

"Jessica Starbuck, and this is my right-hand man, Ki."

The announcement of her name sent a murmur through the crowd as they realized they were in the presence of the Lone Star Legend.

Jessie took the marshal's hand and shook it, but Ki turned his head when the marshal offered his hand to Ki.

"Did you know this man, Miss Starbuck?"

Ki saw Jessie's eyes moisten over. "Yes, Wade Shaw was his name."

Bayless jerked his head toward Jessie. "The Texas Ranger?"

Jessie nodded slightly.

"Damnation," Bayless answered. "Would you two mind coming with me to my office so I can get a few questions answered away from listening ears?"

Ki stepped forward and pointed his finger at the deputy Burton. "We went by your office earlier, trying to let the law know, but the law was playing cards and too busy to do anything else."

The two offending deputies moved back into the crowd.

"Burton, you and Ernest, come here," Bayless commanded. His eyes narrowed as they approached. "That true what the man says?"

Burton grabbed his gunbelt with both hands and pulled it up. "Sort of, but we didn't know it was Jessie Starbuck."

Bayless shook his head. "I don't care who comes to our office for help. Our job is to assist them, not to play cards."

Burton hung his head and Ernest glanced away, both trying to hide the embarrassment of being dressed down before a crowd.

"Burton, you and Ernest, see that an undertaker picks up the body and reports to me on the wounds. Buy a wooden box for him too."

"No," Jessie said, stepping forward. "Buy a fine coffin and bill Starbuck Cotton Exporters. I want the coffin shipped to the capital. I'll let the governor know he's to be buried in the state cemetery."

150

Burton glanced at Ernest. "She really does know the governor."

Jessie turned to Ki. "Let's go with the marshal and see if we can get this taken care of. We've got business to attend to."

Ki knew the business of which she spoke—finding Wade Shaw's killers and bringing them to justice.

Bayless turned to the crowd. "You men get back to work. There's nothing more to see."

"Yeah," yelled Burton, "you heard the marshal. Go on about your business."

Bayless shook his head and pursed his lips as he watched his two deputies at work. He looked at Jessie and offered an apology. "Pay being as low as it is, that's the best I can hire. Would you two come along with me?"

The marshal waited until Jessie and Ki stepped to his side, then moved through the dispersing crowd. He didn't say much until they got to his office. Inside he talked. "I apologize for my deputies not following up on your earlier visit. Now tell me what you know."

Jessie and Ki began the story of The Scorpion, and focused on the incidents of last night. Ki offered the marshal the rope and grappling hook he had found on the hotel balcony and the stiletto the assassin had thrown at Jessie. They offered their suspicions that Lord Clinton Bly was The Scorpion.

"Bly's the one with the yacht down at the pier, isn't he?" asked Bayless.

"He is," answered Ki, "and he may be leaving tomorrow for Mexico."

With his many questions, the marshal kept them past lunch. That was when Ernest and Burton returned with more details on Wade Shaw's death. The undertaker had reported thirteen stab wounds to the chest, plus one in the left shoulder and the scorpion carved on his stomach.

Bayless dispatched Ernest to tell the jail cook to prepare extra meals for himself, Jessie, and Ki.

"What about us?" Ernest asked.

"You two need to head on home and get some sleep before tonight. I want you to guard Lord Clinton Bly's yacht and make sure he doesn't slip away from us. There are some questions he must answer about the Ranger's death.

"One other thing, Burton. I need you to take a message down to the telegraph office."

Burton stepped forward as Bayless grabbed a piece of paper and pencil at his desk. He wrote out a message and handed it to the deputy.

"Why, this is to the gover—"

"I know who it's to, Burton," replied an exasperated marshal. "Just see that it's sent. Then go home and go to bed. It'll be a long night for you."

When the deputies departed, Jessie looked at Bayless. "You don't believe our story, Marshal? Is that why you're sending a message to the governor?"

Bayless pursed his lips, then spoke with carefully measured words. "My job's to get at the truth of the Ranger's death. Had I known of your presence and Shaw's before this happened, these steps would not be necessary. After all, the Ranger was stabbed thirteen times in the chest with a knife." He picked up the stiletto that Ki and Jessie had brought from the hotel. He weighed it in his hand. "I'm just doing my job."

Ki was growing impatient and furious at the delay. He wanted to find Mai Lay before their scheduled rendezvous tonight on the beach. "Are we under arrest?" Ki said with a scowl.

Bayless shook his head. "If you were under arrest, I'd have your weapons and you'd be behind bars."

"Then we're free to go?" Ki shot back.

Bayless offered a weak smile. "Not until I say so. We'll get this settled as soon as we can."

"Be patient, Ki," Jessie said. "When we're cleared with the authorities, we'll get to the bottom of this."

"I thought that was my job," Bayless said.

Ki grumbled. "We thought it was your deputies' job when we first came here this morning, but we were wrong."

152

Bayless shrugged. "I wish I had better help."

"We're offering you the best help you'll ever get," Ki said.

"And I'll accept your help when the time is right."

When the jail cook brought them lunch, Bayless made room on the corner of his desk for Jessie and Ki to place their tin plates ladled with boiled beans, ham hocks, and a slab of cornbread slathered with butter.

Ki ate because he had nothing else to do right now, but he noticed Jessie mostly toyed with her food. She was still distraught over Shaw's death.

As the afternoon wore on, Ki waited as patiently as he could. Bayless issued a request for a judge's order to keep Bly from leaving the port on his yacht. He had another deputy deliver that request, then sat and waited.

Ki figured he would wait until dark for Bayless to release them. If the marshal didn't let him go, Ki would take matters into his own hands because he had to meet Mai Lay. And once it was dark, he could more easily slip aboard Bly's yacht.

Just about dusk, Bayless received two messages. One was a telegram from the capital. Bayless ripped open the yellow envelope and began to skim the long message. "It's from the governor," Bayless said. He began to shake his head. "Your story holds up. In fact, the governor says we are to provide around-the-clock protection for you, Miss Starbuck, until a company of Texas Rangers gets to Galveston. Seems like Galveston is the base for some Mexican gun smuggling."

Ki stood up from his chair and moved to the door, stretching his muscles.

"Where you going?" Bayless asked.

"The governor didn't say anything about *me* being guarded all the time. While you're sitting here trying to figure out what to do, I'll be doing something."

Bayless lifted his hand. "Hold up a moment." He skimmed the telegram again. "You're right, nothing here says we've got to protect you."

Ki nodded to Bayless, then Jessie.

153

"But before you go, let me read the response from the judge." The marshal took the paper and looked it over, smiling as he did. "We've been granted the papers to keep Lord Bly and his yacht in port for three days. We should be able to get to the bottom of this by then."

Jessie looked at Ki. "I hope you find out what you need to know and what you want to know from Mai Lay."

Ki tried desperately to hide his emotions, but knew he had failed. She had been around him long enough to know the meaning of the slightest change in his expression or his temperament.

"We'll serve the papers on Bly," Bayless said, "then take our turns guarding Miss Starbuck's hotel room."

Ki went quickly out the door. The daylight was fading and it was cool, with another bank of fog rolling in. Ki moved quickly down the street, taking a circuitous route to lose anyone who might be following him.

As dusk turned into night, Ki stood at the far end of the docks, then started toward the wooden ribs of a ship grounded years ago in a storm. The ribs stood out from the beach like the bones of a great extinct water monster. He was soon standing beneath the skeleton that was all that remained from the once-proud ship.

Ki waited. He had so many questions to ask Mai Lay. As the time dragged by and Galveston itself was shrouded in fog until all that was visible was a giant glow in the mist, Ki began to walk around the wrecked hull. He lingered until ten o'clock, then another hour more, all the time wondering what Mai Lay's role was in all of this. She had escaped the sailors who had attacked her in the stable last night only because Wade Shaw's chase of The Scorpion had distracted them. Did she run naked to the ship? How could she know it was Wade Shaw who ran past? After all, Wade had crossed the street before he passed the stable, and the fog was thick last night, too thick to identify people with certainty. If Wade Shaw were killed aboard Bly's yacht, then was Mai Lay likely on it at the time? What did she know about his death? And what

154

about the guard with the eye patch? Wasn't he the same sailor who had followed Jessie and Ki from the train station upon their arrival? Wasn't he one of the four men who had assaulted Bly and Mai Lay by the stables? Was that a setup so Jessie and Ki would underestimate Bly's cunning?

And most of all, what did Mai Lay know about The Scorpion?

From the piers, Ki heard a shrill steam whistle. In the murky air, the whistle came from all directions, but Ki knew that it was the whistle on Bly's yacht, the whistle he had heard last night. Then it came back to him. First he had heard a terrible scream, which was instantly drowned out by the steam whistle. Ki caught his breath as his mind began to review the events of last night. The scream was surely Wade Shaw being tortured before his death.

Ki stopped dead in his tracks. Now it made sense. Mai Lay was a decoy whose mission it was to distract Ki from Jessie while The Scorpion attacked. Then Ki had a sinking feeling. He had been decoyed again. Mai Lay would not be showing up tonight. She had suggested this meeting place only to get him away from Jessie.

And it had worked!

Ki bolted toward town. He had to get to the hotel before it was too late. He ran as hard as he could, but the sandy beach seemed to suck at his feet and impede his every stride. Finally reaching the road, he ran as the wind, his heart pounding as much from the fear of finding Jessie harmed as from the exertion.

Racing past the few people on the street, he drew their curious stares or spooked their animals, but was so quickly lost in the fog that they didn't even have time to curse. He raced along the docks, then turned up the side street beside the Crown Hotel and darted around the front, under the portico, and inside the crowded lobby. He dodged the paths and the stares of several men and women, then bounded up the stairs and down the hall toward his room and Jessie's Grand Suite.

155

He caught his breath. The deputy unconscious on the floor outside Jessie's door confirmed his suspicions. The Scorpion had visited in his absence. The door to Jessie's room was wide open and in the bedroom, Ki found Marshal Bayless on his hands and knees, shaking his head. On Jessie's bed, Ki saw her .38-caliber revolver where it had been discarded. Since he couldn't find her derringer on the bed or on the floor around it, he hoped she still had it.

Ki grabbed the marshal's shoulders and shook him. He groaned and grimaced as he looked up at Ki.

"What happened?" Ki demanded.

Bayless shook his head again. "Some black-clad little fellow broke in and knocked me out. Where's Miss Starbuck?"

"Gone with The Scorpion to Bly's yacht," Ki guessed.

Bayless spat out a few bitter words as he rubbed his head. "The Scorpion's a mean little son of a bitch."

"That describes Bly," Ki shouted, "and I've got to get him before he hurts Jessie."

Ki turned for the door.

"What can I do?" Bayless called after him.

"Get all the men you can to the pier."

"I got two there already."

"You'll need more to stop The Scorpion."

Ki darted out the door, raced down the stairs two steps at a time, and then shot through the lobby again. He was out on the street instantly and sprinting past the Crown, down the side street, and toward the pier. He heard the steam whistle again, and then the noise of men on the docks.

Up ahead, a ghostly shape began to come into focus out of the fog. It was Bly's yacht. The side paddle wheels were turning. The yacht was pulling away from the dock.

Ki didn't know if he could make it in time to get aboard before the paddle steamer moved from its slip out into the bay. He ran harder. Had he watched over Jessie all these years to lose her like this? He cursed himself for thinking too much of Mai Lay and too little of Jessie.

★

Chapter 18

It had happened so quickly that Jessie could not reconstruct in her mind exactly what had taken place. She was resting on her bed, thinking about the loss of Wade Shaw and worrying for Ki's safety, when she heard the door open. She thought nothing of it since a deputy was outside and the marshal himself was on the balcony. She had a key and the deputy outside had a key. Then everything was quiet, unnaturally quiet.

"Marshal?" she called, her hand reaching for her .38-caliber revolver.

Then out of the corner of her eye, she saw a figure clad from head to toe in black. The figure was upon her instantly, knocking the gun to the bed with a chop of her hand, then using a stranglehold upon her. Jessie remembered thinking The Scorpion had returned for her, and she realized Wade Shaw had been carrying a key to her room when he died. The Scorpion had taken that key. She wished for Ki, and then she passed out.

When she awoke she was gagged and bound to a chair. There was total darkness, and for a moment she was uncertain if she were awake or asleep. She tried to collect her senses, clear her head of the unanswered questions about her abduction. She had to figure out where she was. She suspected she was aboard Bly's yacht and she listened intently. A shrill steam whistle exploded from nearby and answered her question. She was in a windowless room somewhere in Bly's steamship. The room reeked of grease and metal shavings and oil, but she could be certain of nothing else.

Gradually her senses perceived the slight rocking of the room and the noises of the waterfront. She wondered if this was the same room where Wade Shaw had met his death. Would a similar fate await her here? Jessie struggled against the ropes binding her legs, chest, and arms to a chair and her hands to each other. They were tight and would not give. In anger, Jessie bit against the cloth in her mouth, trying to gnaw it in half, but nothing worked.

Damn Lord Clinton Bly, she thought.

Outside her room, she could hear the sounds of feet running along the teak deck and the calls of men giving orders, as if they were preparing to cast off from shore. Jessie knew if the ship ever left Galveston, her chances of survival were nil. She struggled harder against the ropes and the gag, but they were too strong and she was too tired. As she moved her leg, she thought she could feel the derringer still in her garter holster. That was the only advantage she could identify for herself, and it was only a two-shot advantage. The only other thing she had going for her was Ki. Somewhere he was out there, and he would not rest until he had rescued her or died trying.

Jessie heard the noise of men outside the room, then the clang of a metal handle and the groan of a heavy door swinging open on iron hinges. A patch of light appeared on the wall opposite her and though the light was soft, it was hard upon her eyes. She squinted, and just made out the shadow of one man, then another passing through the light. They strode to her and stood on opposite sides of the chair. Without a word, they bent, grabbed the chair by the legs and back, and lifted it and Jessie from the floor. In the dim light, Jessie was now able to see she had been held prisoner in the ship's tool room. She looked at the two sailors. Both were

158

compact and powerful. The one to her left wore a patch over his eye, and Jessie remembered him from the train station and from the robbery attempt on Lord Clinton Bly and Mai Lay. Now she was really confused.

They carried her out into the bright iron hallway, then toward the ship's bow, before entering a hallway beneath the bridge. They took her into a wide, well-lit room. Jessie had to squint at the brightness, and then gritted her teeth against the gag in her mouth. There in a deep leather chair sat Lord Clinton Bly. Jessie could not stand the sight of him and turned away, taking in the large bed in the center and the huge desk to the side.

"Welcome, good lady," Bly said as he stood up and bowed. "Such a pity you did not accept my offer to buy all Starbuck cotton. You are as stubborn as your father was."

Jessie was disgusted at the mention of her father by a man so vile.

Bly instructed one of the sailors to remove her gag. "Let her yell all she wants. We'll be casting off shortly and there's not a thing she can do to protect herself now."

Not, Jessie thought, unless she could get her hands on her derringer. If she were going to die, she could at least take Lord Clinton Bly with her.

The man with the patch pulled a knife, leered at her for a moment with his single eye, then slipped the flat of the knife between Jessie's cheek and the gag. Jessie could feel the cold of the steel blade against her, but she refused to show fear. If she was going to die, she would die bravely like her father. The sailor twisted the blade's sharpness against the gag and sliced it free. Jessie spat the cloth from her mouth.

Jessie remembered this evil man with the eye patch. "Isn't this the man that tried to rob you?" Jessie asked.

Bly laughed. "Indeed he was, good lady, but it was mere theater. I was never in danger. We just wanted you to think so, a way of introducing ourselves from a weakened posture so you would underestimate our strength. You see, good lady,

159

my short stature has made me a stronger man. People assume I can't be strong if I'm short. You thought I was impotent after the theatrical robbery.

"And the hotel room? What they call the Grand Suite was anything but that, good lady, but I rented it just so I could be a grand fellow and turn it over to you. And so I could have an extra key in case we needed to enter." Bly stuck his hand in his pocket and pulled out a key.

"Of course, we needn't have wasted the effort had we known your boorish Ranger friend would be carrying one when we dispatched him."

Jessie rocked in her chair, the anger surging through her veins. She wished she could reach her derringer. "You monster."

"Monster? Me? Why, no, good lady. I'm just an industrialist trying to take care of my business as economically as possible."

"Industrialists don't kill."

Bly lifted his hands in surprise and offered Jessie a look of mock hurt. "I did not kill your rude friend. I did not want to get my hands dirty, but I must say I enjoyed seeing him die. He screamed until the moment of his passing, The Scorpion being good in ways of making death agonizing."

"So you are The Scorpion?"

Bly let his hands fall to his waist. "Good lady, I did not say that. I said I enjoyed seeing him die. He treated me rudely. Two times he refused my generous offers of meals. Twice he spurned me." Bly stepped toward Jessie. "You've spurned my offer to buy your cotton. That wasn't a wise thing to do. I don't like to be refused. The meals for the Ranger, well, those are small mistakes and I allow two small mistakes. But the cotton deal, now that was a big mistake, and I don't allow but one of those.

"And, good lady, it'll be the last mistake you'll ever make. Once you're dead, I'll buy out the Starbuck cotton business and get my wish anyway."

Jessie lifted her chin defiantly. "Not as long as Martin Bark is in charge. He warned me about you as soon as I got to Galveston."

"Yes, good lady, but we both know Bark is nearing retirement. He wouldn't be around long whether or not I dispatch him."

Jessie was amazed that Bly knew so much about her people and business. He was an insidious man, one who would let nothing stand in his way of achieving his crazed plans.

"Are you a remnant of the cartel?"

Bly laughed, almost maniacally. "They approached me at one point and I would've assisted them, but at the meeting we had, they laughed at my height and mocked me. After that they didn't want me, and I didn't want anything to do with them except to destroy them. That was what your father and I had in common. We wanted to destroy the cartel."

Jessie shook her head. "You had nothing in common with my father. He did it for the good of mankind. You were against them only so you could take over their evil designs."

Bly stroked his chin and began to circle Jessie's chair. "It's easy for such a small man as me to slip into such a large void, especially with the help of The Scorpion. The Ranger was The Scorpion's nineteenth sting," he bragged.

He was a sick man, Jessie thought, referring to The Scorpion in the third person rather than as himself.

"You, good lady, will be The Scorpion's twentieth sting, but we shall wait until we get to Mexico, where The Scorpion will rejoin us."

Was he so deranged that he thought of The Scorpion as some other person who traveled a separate road doing his dirty work? Jessie had never encountered someone so deliriously evil. Oh, how right Wade Shaw's suspicions had been, and Jessie rued not having paid more attention to them. Had she done so, Wade might still be alive.

"Why Mexico?"

"Good lady, you are so naive that you cannot understand. Mexico is politically unstable. All it needs is the right person to confuse the politics and its troubles will overflow into Texas and the United States. This very ship is loaded with guns and explosives to help stir up things. I have no doubt that the colonies, as they still should be, will triumph over such a lesser country in the case of a conflict, but your government and your Army will be distracted and I can . . ."

Jessie finished for him. "Do your evil will?"

"Tsk, tsk, tsk," Bly said. "That was not nearly how I would have stated it, good lady."

"I will do everything in my power to stop you, Bly," Jessie challenged.

Lord Bly cocked his head and looked strangely at her. "Do you understand how ridiculous that sounds? You sit before me bound and helpless, subject to my pleasures and whims." He walked to her and took a handful of her copper-blond hair in his hand. "This is a ship loaded with sailors and hard men, good lady. Already some have come to me offering a month's wages to do with you what they want." He jerked her hair until her head was twisted to the side of the room where the two sailors stood. "Ain't that right, boys?"

The one-eyed sailor and his companion both nodded.

"But, good lady, I am a gentleman. I said no, and anyone who tries to take advantage of you will die." He smiled. "Now, I give you this warning. If you try anything on our journey, I'll turn you over to the sailors until there's nothing left of you but fish bait." He released her hair and walked away.

"You are a desperate man, Bly."

"But not nearly as desperate as you are. You have a rendezvous with death. I have a rendezvous with destiny."

There was a knock on the door, and the two sailors moved in unison to answer it.

"Lord Bly," said the voice of a sailor Jessie could not see, "we are preparing to cast off."

"Very well, men."

"You're violating a judge's order to stay in port," Jessie challenged, knowing it was foolish to argue with him, but knowing there was nothing else she could do as long as she was bound.

"And I'm violating the law by abducting you," he said, folding his arms across his chest, "but great men stay great only by taking risks, good lady."

"Desperate men take great risks," she shot back.

Bly laughed. "Be contentious and courageous while you can, good lady, because once we leave the pier you are on the last trip you will ever take on this earth. By the time we reach Mexico, we'll see how brave you are."

Bly ordered the two sailors in the room to take up their posts for departure. Then he moved over to his desk and took a chair. He wrote out something, then brought it to Jessie and held it in front of her eyes.

She recognized the paper as the same type that she and Wade Shaw had found under her door with a representation of a scorpion drawn on it. She read what was a simple contract giving power of attorney over the Starbuck empire to Lord Clinton Bly.

"Never," she said.

"You'll have to reconsider the closer we get to Mexico."

Outside Jessie heard the slap of the twin paddle wheels hitting water. The great yacht began to move. She wondered if she would ever stand on Texas soil again.

★
Chapter 19

The paddle steamer began to pull away from the dock. Ki ran harder than he thought possible, thinking at first he might be able to jump from the dock and grab onto something to shimmy up the side of the ship. But what?

By the time he reached the end of the dock, the yacht had pulled too far away and there was nothing to grab. He glanced down the dock and caught a glimpse of the two deputy marshals, Burton and Ernest, who were sprawled on the wood where they had been knocked unconscious.

Once the steamer cleared the end of the dock, it could pick up speed and he could never catch her. Ki ran to the edge of the dock. He was quickly running out of options.

Then he saw a dinghy tethered to a piling. He jumped from the dock into the boat, pulled his *tanto* from its sheath, and sliced the tether rope. Tossing his curved knife into the boat, he shoved against the piling to gather some momentum, then grabbed the two paddles, shoved them in the oar locks, and began to paddle with full, complete strokes, looking over his shoulder as the yacht inched toward the bay.

Ki was gaining on it, but he doubted he could catch it before it passed the end of the pier and turned out into the bay. He pulled harder, screaming with the exertion, but even if he caught up with it, how could he climb on board? He thought he might be able to ride one of the giant revolving paddles up, but he knew he could never reach the paddles. They were in the middle of the steamer, and he would be lucky to draw up to the stern.

Paddling furiously, he let each stroke pull deeply in the water so he could gather as much speed as possible. He was gaining because the steamer still had not cleared the dock, but the yacht's paddles had passed and Ki knew he didn't have much time. When he was within twenty-five feet of the yacht's stern, he knew he was running out of options. He wished he had the rope and grappling hook The Scorpion had used to get into Jessie's hotel room. He pulled within twenty feet of the yacht, then fifteen, before he thought of the dinghy's anchor rope. With one final gigantic pull on the oars, he released them and they banged against the side of the dinghy as he scrambled up front and grabbed the small mud anchor that was in the middle of a coil of rope.

Taking the anchor, which weighed three pounds maximum, he twirled it over his head, letting out a little rope at a time. If only he had enough rope! If only he tied onto something on his first throw! He would not have a second chance because he could not retrieve the anchor before the yacht pulled out of range. He had to succeed. Jessie's life depended on it!

As the anchor came around his shoulder a final time, he released it for the deck railing. He held his breath. The anchor seemed to take forever to arch through the sky, and all the time the yacht was pulling away. Then the anchor started falling. Ki bit his lip. The anchor landed over the deck railing and caught. The rope went instantly taut from the steamer's momentum, then jerked the dinghy forward. Ki tumbled backward onto the seat. He didn't care, though, because the boat was clinging by rope to the yacht.

From the ship, he heard the shouts of men who heard a noise they couldn't explain. As he crawled back to the front of the boat he found the *tanto* he had tossed aside earlier, and slid it into the sheath at his waistband. At the front of the boat, which trailed maybe fifty feet behind the yacht, he began to pull in part of the anchor line so he could draw close enough to the yacht to climb the rope and board. As the steamer moved out into the bay, the fog got thicker, and the dinghy seemed to be skimming through the water much too fast for such poor visibility.

It was exhausting work tugging his boat closer to the ship, and when he was within twenty feet of the yacht, he saw a sailor stop near the railing where the anchor had hooked. The sailor seemed to understand something was amiss, and put down his rifle and reached with both hands to unravel the anchor and line from the railing. Ki had to act fast. With his left hand and arm straining to hold on to the anchor rope and not lose any of the ground he had gained, his right fell to the nearest pocket of his vest and pulled out a throwing star. The dinghy was bouncing like a bucking bull, making the throw all the more difficult. Ki thought of Jessie and grew all the more determined. He drew his arm back behind his ear and flung the *shuriken* with a flick of his wrist.

Instantly, Ki grabbed the line with both hands and started pulling harder to reach the ship. He saw the sailor suddenly release the anchor rope and grab for his throat. The sailor teetered for a moment, then toppled onto the deck. Ki didn't have much time now. The next sailor to pass would know something was amiss. Within ten feet of the yacht, Ki took a breath, pushed himself off from the boat, and swung for the yacht. The dinghy dropped behind him as he swayed forward, but he had not closed near enough to the ship to avoid the water. His legs dragged in the waves, and he scrambled to pull himself out. Then the dinghy behind him hit the end of the rope and the rope rose slightly out of the water, giving him a chance to wrap both legs around it and continue his climb. Finally, he pulled himself close enough that he swung against the yacht's iron hull. Then he lifted his feet against the iron sheath and, with his arms providing the leverage, began to walk up the side of the yacht. No sooner had he grabbed onto the railing itself than another sailor ran up, pausing to pull a pistol from his holster and fire at Ki.

Ki scrambled over the railing and rolled across the deck wet with the first sailor's blood. Ki grabbed the downed sailor's rifle, bounced to his feet, and rushed the pistol-toting sailor. He lifted the rifle over his head and swung it like a club for the latest assailant, cracking him solidly against the forehead. Man and pistol fell to the deck. Instantly, Ki kicked his pistol over the edge into the water, then flung the rifle away as well.

He retreated a moment and secured the dinghy line. He knew he would need the boat to make his escape. He shoved the two injured men overboard so they could not raise an alarm. Now he had to find Jessie fast because, once the yacht got out of the bay, his and Jessie's chances for survival diminished.

Then he ran forward on the deck toward an open cargo hold and the paddle wheels. He saw the flash of a gun, then heard the explosion. He dove to the deck and the bullet pinged off an iron cowl. He saw another sailor running in his direction along the deck. The sailor, though, didn't seem to spot Ki until he was right upon him. Ki shot up and stopped the sailor with a fist to the groin. He doubled over and Ki fell atop him, just as another bullet whizzed overhead.

"Where's the woman?" Ki screamed as he grabbed the man around the neck. "Tell me."

The man gasped for breath. "In Bly's quarters."

"Where's that?"

"Under the bridge," he managed.

Ki took the rifle the man had dropped and tossed it overboard. "Stand up and run," Ki ordered, "or I'll kill you."

The desperate sailor tried to get to his feet. It was the distraction Ki needed to dash down the deck. The wobbly sailor took two bullets, screamed, and collapsed beside the cargo hold.

Ki darted between ventilator cowls and winches and other deck obstacles as he made his way toward the bridge. He darted into a passageway just as another sailor turned the corner. As the sailor stepped by the darkened doorway, Ki clubbed him on the neck so he dropped his rifle, then grabbed him under the arms and rammed his head against the steel side. The man fell like dirty clothes in a heap.

He moved deeper into the ship until he came to a lighted hallway that looked more elegant than anything he had yet seen. He had to be nearing Bly's quarters. He slid another throwing star out of his vest and cocked his hand. On deck, Ki could hear panicked commotion as orders were issued and lamps lit to begin an inch-by-inch search for him. He moved deeper into the passageway. All of a sudden a door swung open and a man with a patch over his eye jumped out in the hallway with a pistol. He fired just as Ki flung the *shuriken* at him and jumped for the wall. The bullet sliced through a fold in his shirt without scratching Ki, then bounced off the steel walls until it fell spent to the floor. The sailor who had plagued them since they had set foot in Galveston slapped at his good eye where the star had impaled itself, then collapsed in a quivering mass on the floor.

Ki grabbed another throwing star and eased down the hallway toward the open door.

"In here, Ki! There's two of them."

"Shut up," said a voice Ki didn't recognize. Then came the snap of a hand slapping flesh.

Jessie cried out, then yelled another warning. "One's by the door, Bly's at the back of the room."

Ki caught his breath, ran down the hall, and dove through the door. A gun exploded over Ki's flying body. Ki hit the floor and rolled over, then spun around and flung his *shuriken* at the sailor by the door. The sailor dropped his gun and stared wide-eyed at the flower of blood blossoming on his shirt.

By his desk Lord Clinton Bly stood bewildered, his eyes transfixed on the dying sailor's bloody chest. He held a gun limply at his side and seemed terrified.

Ki charged toward him, but Bly never moved, just stood

there as if he had seen death face-to-face for the first time. Ki grabbed Bly's limp wrist and jerked the gun from his hand, then glanced at Jessie.

"You okay?"

"I am now that you're here."

"We're not safe yet and won't be until we're off this ship. Keep an eye on him while I cut you free." Ki pulled the *tanto* from his waistband and sliced through the ropes binding her legs and arms to the chair. Then he slit the ropes on her wrists.

Jessie rubbed her hands and arms, then her legs. She tried to stand, but was wobbly.

"Rest a bit longer and hold this," Ki instructed as he handed Jessie Bly's revolver.

Bly was pale.

"You're not so brave when someone has the upper hand, are you, Scorpion?" Jessie said.

He quivered as she lifted the gun.

Ki quickly shut the iron door, and then closed the metal hatches around the stateroom to keep sailors from sniping at them. He turned to Jessie. "Getting here was the easy part. Getting off will be hard, especially if the yacht gets out in the Gulf."

Watching Jessie, Ki saw as steely a glint as he had ever seen in her green eyes.

"He deserves to die, but he's our only ticket to freedom. He can order the ship back to port," she said.

Ki shook his head. "No, the captain would just keep on going. So what if we killed him. No, we've got to use him as a shield and get off the ship. I've got a dinghy trailing us." Then Ki had an idea. It was desperate, but it was their only chance of survival. He jumped for Bly and slapped him hard across the face. The industrialist seemed to come back to reality. Ki grabbed him by the scruff of the neck and moved him to the door, opening it slightly.

"Tell your crew you're okay," Ki commanded.

"Men," he started. Then Ki tightened his grip on Bly's

169

neck and lifted the curved blade of the *tanto* under his chin.

"Louder," Ki scowled.

"Men," yelled Bly, "I'm safe, so back away and give us some room."

"That's better," Ki said in his ear. "Now tell them to bring three lit lanterns into the hall outside your door, then back away."

"Somebody bring three lit lanterns to my door, then clear the area," Bly said.

One of the sailors obliged, and the passageway fairly glowed with lamplight.

Ki looked over his shoulder at Jessie. "Think you can walk now?"

Jessie rose slowly, and was a bit gimpy when she took a step. "We're running out of time." She wobbled to Ki.

"Keep the gun on him and shoot him if he doesn't obey our orders." Ki felt Bly tremble.

"Now listen, your lordship, you announce to your men we're coming out and you're our shield. You grab a lantern in each hand and hold them out where you can light our way."

"Don't shoot. They're using me as a shield," Bly announced, his voice trembling with fear. "Don't shoot."

Ki opened the door and kept his hand on Bly's neck. The industrialist bent and picked up two lanterns before stepping out the door. Ki poked his head out, making sure there was no ambush. The hall was clear. He stepped outside and placed the knife beneath Bly's chin. "Jessie, grab the other lantern."

"Damn, Ki, you want to make sure we're well lit enough to pick us off?"

"No," Ki said, "I want one of the lamps to throw in the cargo hold and start a fire. They'll have to fight it instead of worrying about us."

"You fool," Bly screamed. "You know what's in the hold? Dynamite and explosives."

Ki poked the knife into Bly's flesh until it drew blood.

"Listen, your lordship, if anybody tries anything, Jessie'll throw a lantern in the hold, you understand?"

"No," Bly pleaded.

"Then let your men know."

"He's crazy, men. They'll throw a lamp on the explosives if we try anything," Bly shouted. "Stay back, don't do a thing."

Ki eased Bly down the passageway to the open door that led onto the deck. Jessie followed behind them, the gun at the ready.

They slipped out onto the deck and advanced along the railing toward the middle of the steamer and the cargo hold. All around the well-lit deck Ki could see sailors armed and ready to kill him.

"They'll blow us up," Bly screamed, "if you try anything. Just let them go and don't let me get hurt. I'll double the wages of every man on this ship. Just don't start any shooting."

No one said a thing as Ki and Jessie, their backs to the railing and the bay waters, edged ever closer and closer to the stern. Passing the revolving paddle wheel, they were sprinkled with water.

They made it past the paddle wheel, but the clump of sailors on the opposite side of the ship moved parallel to them. Ki knew he and Jessie would have little chance of survival if the ship stayed afloat. Ki slipped his hand around Bly's neck and covered the Englishman's mouth. "Listen to me, Jessie," Ki whispered as he lowered his knife hand to Bly's hand and took a lantern from him. "See the open cargo hold?"

"Yes," she replied.

"When I count three, throw your lantern into it."

"What?" Jessie called.

Desperate for his life, Bly began to squirm and try to sound the warning.

"Just do it, dammit, it's our only chance. Then follow me to the stern."

"What then?" she asked.

171

"That's where the dinghy's tied. I'll show you the rope. You hang onto it while I cut it loose and pull yourself to the boat. I'll find you in the water."

"It's foggy," she said.

"It doesn't matter," Ki answered, "because it's our only chance." He started counting off. "One."

Bly struggled and tried to scream.

Ki managed to keep his mouth covered. "Two."

Jessie drew back her lantern.

"Three," Ki yelled.

Jessie flung her lantern into the open cargo hold. The sound of shattering glass was followed by the whoosh of coal oil taking to blaze.

Instantly, Ki flung his lantern at the clump of sailors opposite him. The lantern fell short, but the blaze blinded them long enough for Ki to shove Bly toward the back, Jessie running beside him.

Terrified, Bly flailed and tried to get free. Ki let him have his wish, shoving him hard to the deck. Bly screamed and tumbled on the teak deck, then landed atop the lantern he'd dropped. There was an explosion of flame beneath his stomach. Then he cried in terror as flames engulfed him.

Ki pulled Jessie down the deck. All was pandemonium now, several men shooting their weapons, some trying to fight the fires. At the back of the ship, he found where he had tied the dinghy. "Over the railing and hang on to this rope until I cut it," he commanded Jessie.

As she climbed outside the railing, several sailors charged for them. She emptied the revolver at them, two falling down and a couple more retreating for cover. Jessie flung the revolver into the Gulf, then grabbed the rope and let herself slide out over the water.

"It'll be cold," Ki yelled, "but hang on to the rope." He lifted the curved blade of the *tanto* and sliced the rope. For an instant he saw Jessie. Then she disappeared. Ki shoved the knife in the sheath in his waistband and dove over the railing, just as several sailors fired at him. Ki plunged headlong into

172

the frigid water. For an instant, it took his breath away. Then he clambered to the surface and began sputtering water and swimming away from the yacht.

"Jessie," he yelled. "Are you okay, did you hang on to the rope?"

"Yes," she called back, "I can see the boat."

As they yelled, the yacht plunged on, its decks lit by fires that made a strange glow as the vessel grew murky in the fog.

"Hang on, Ki," Jessie yelled in a few minutes. "I just pulled myself in the boat."

By yelling back and forth, Ki was eventually able to direct Jessie to him. She rowed beside him and he grabbed an oar, then worked his way to the back of the dinghy, where he drew himself aboard.

"Are you okay, Jessie."

"Wet and cold, but alive."

They huddled next to one another, shivering together as they watched the indistinct glow in the fog. Then all at once, the glow mushroomed into a ball of flame and a giant explosion rippled through the air toward them.

Neither Ki nor Jessie said anything for a few minutes. They didn't need to. They both knew they had destroyed an evil man and they were both proud of it, especially after what he had done to Wade Shaw. Ki wondered about Mai Lay, and was glad that he had not encountered her on the yacht because he could not have abandoned her, even if she did work for such a dastardly man.

Then Ki took the oars from Jessie, maneuvered the dinghy around as best he could tell in the fog, and started the long row back to Galveston. With a bit of luck, the rising tide, and three hours of strained muscles, Ki made it to the piers of Galveston. A crowd of folks drawn by the explosion still stood at the docks, Marshal Bayless among them. He met Jessie and Ki and escorted them to his office to review everything that had occurred since Jessie was abducted from her room.

★

Chapter 20

By the time they finished with the legal details in the marshal's office, it was almost dawn. Marshal Bayless thanked them profusely for stopping Lord Clinton Bly, then saw that a carriage was available to take them back to the Crown Hotel for deserved rest. He said he would telegraph the governor the details, then noted that Wade Shaw's body had been sent to the capital as Jessie had requested.

Ki watched Jessie, knowing she was still taking Shaw's loss hard. He wished there were something he could do for her, but he could do nothing except sympathize. After all, he had lost Mai Lay, and lost her under less honorable circumstances. Jessie asked the marshal to deliver a message to Martin Bark at Starbuck Cotton Exporters to wire the Circle Star and have her Pullman car sent to Galveston for the return trip. The marshal agreed, then escorted Ki and Jessie to the carriage when it arrived.

Lost in their thoughts and their exhaustion, Jessie and Ki rode wordlessly to the hotel. They nodded to the driver as they slid out of the carriage and entered the hotel. After leaving a message at the desk that their rooms were not to be disturbed until further notice, Jessie and Ki retired upstairs. Though Jessie's key had been taken during her abduction, Ki had his and opened his door, figuring to let her go out onto the balcony and into her room by the balcony door.

They entered, and Ki locked the door behind them. The room was bathed in the soft light of dawn. As Ki led Jessie toward the balcony door he heard a stirring in the bed, and was startled when the sheet moved. There was someone in his room and in his bed! His hand flew to his vest for a *shuriken* as the dimly lit body ran to him.

"Ki, you're okay!"

Ki recognized Mai Lay's voice, and then her naked body as she threw her arms around him. She kissed him hard upon the lips, then broke away with a flurry of explanations.

"He made me lie to you, distract you while he abducted Miss Starbuck." She looked past Ki to Jessie, and seemed shocked by her presence. Mai Lay backed away to the bed and pulled the sheet free to wrap around her nakedness. "I'm sorry, Miss Starbuck, about your friend the Ranger."

Jessie nodded.

Then Mai Lay turned back to Ki. "I tried to meet you on the beach and let you know, but Lord Bly kept me under guard. I managed to slip free and came back here to warn you Miss Starbuck had been taken, but I couldn't find you and the yacht departed."

Ki stood in shock. He had given Mai Lay up for dead, and yet here she stood before him. It was unbelievable. And she had tried to warn him about Jessie's capture. She had a conscience after all. He moved to her and hugged her through the sheet.

Jessie nodded. "You two have a lot to discuss. I'll let myself in through the balcony."

Ki heard her leave. Then he stepped back from Mai Lay. She teased him as she let the sheet slide slowly away to reveal one breast, then the other. Ki took in her body hungrily as the sheet dropped past her navel and then to her waist and the patch of black down narrowly trimmed between her legs. In the dim light, he could just see the outline of the black mole or a scar on her mound. When she finally released the sheet,

175

it fell to her ankles and she stood there in all her naked glory, an open invitation for Ki. Her long hair was pinned in buns atop her head. Ki wished she would release her hair so that it dropped over her body like a tantalizing veil, but he was too tired to ask.

He started to fumble with his vest, but Mai Lay came to him and slid the vest off his arms, then tossed it across the room. She grabbed his shirt at the bottom and pulled it over his head and let it drop to the floor. As she worked to pull his pants down, she felt the *tanto* sheathed in his waistband, and gently removed it and carried it to the bureau across the room. When she returned, she stripped his trousers over his ankle-high boots before removing them and his socks.

Though he was exhausted, Ki could feel his desire rising like the sun outside.

"Come," she said, taking his arm and guiding him to the bed. "I will treat you as you have never been treated before."

Ki sat down on the bed and she pushed him over on his back, then took his legs and lifted them with her powerful arms onto the mattress. She caressed him briefly, then straddled his waist and pushed herself around him and began to ride his manhood. Unlike their first consummation, this was not love as an art but love as relief. She pounded furiously against him. Ki reached for her firm breasts and took them, but she brushed his hands aside.

"Enjoy," she said.

His arms went limp as he exploded within her, and yet she bucked still harder against him until it seemed her passion would kill him. Ki was spent. She leaned forward on him, until her hardened nipples touched his chest. She placed her lips against his.

"You will never have better," she said.

Ki didn't know about that, but he didn't care just right now. He wanted sleep.

Mai Lay whispered in his ear. "Do you want my hair down?"

Ki nodded.

Mai Lay smiled and pulled herself away from his shrinking desire, sliding up over his stomach to his chest, trailing his spent passion upon his flesh as she moved. She sat straight upon him, lifting her hands to her head.

Ki smiled, glancing from her lips to her breasts, then down her firm stomach to her neatly trimmed bush. The glow of the morning light allowed him to see the black mark upon her mound. It was not a mole after all, but a tattoo.

A tattoo of a scorpion!

For an instant, he did not make the connection. Then he looked up into her now-serious eyes. With each hand, she gently pulled long hairpins from each side of the tightly wrapped buns of her hair.

There was something vaguely familiar about those wide hairpins. They were like the stiletto that had been thrown at Jessie in the first attempt on her life.

Mai Lay was The Scorpion!

She seemed to read his mind. She nodded, then screamed as she started the twin stilettos for his chest.

With what strength he had left, Ki bucked his hips, throwing her off balance. The stilettos sliced past Ki's head, burying themselves in his pillow and the mattress.

Ki shoved her off and bounded out of bed onto his feet, but Mai Lay was so quick she seemed to beat him to the floor. She circled him, waiving both stilettos at him. Ki shook his head. Now so much made sense. Somehow she had learned the way of the *ninja*. "You were never attacked by sailors. It was you that knocked me out at the stable and attacked Jessie and Wade Shaw up here." It came back to Ki now. "You had on the clothes of the *ninja* beneath your kimono."

Mai Lay nodded as she circled him in a prelude to death.

"Why?" Ki asked.

"I am bound to my master just as you are bound to yours by traditions of the *ninjutsu*."

Ki could not argue that. "You killed Wade Shaw."

Mai Lay nodded. "And now I must kill you. I don't care to, but I must."

Ki lunged for her, but she was so quick she leaped away and Ki's hands closed around little but air. Now Ki knew she was skilled in the deadly arts. How a woman had learned them he did not know. He just hoped he had the strength to protect himself.

Though Jessie knew she should be happy for Ki, she was somehow troubled by Mai Lay's reappearance. Jessie walked across the balcony and let herself into the Grand Suite. She made her way to the bed. There on the mattress was her .38-caliber revolver, which The Scorpion had knocked out of her hand during the abduction. On the dresser she saw the folded stationery with the representation of a scorpion upon it. For some reason she picked it up and studied it, then threw it down on the bed beside her revolver.

Her clothes were still damp from the jump in the bay waters, so she took off her vest. From the next room, she heard the sounds of lovemaking and she was jealous. Ki still had Mai Lay, but she no longer had Wade Shaw. Mai Lay must be taken with Ki for her to have to come back to let him know Jessie had been abducted.

Jessie stopped cold as she started to unbutton her blouse. "Wait a minute!" Jessie said aloud to herself. "What did she mean by *come back*?" Jessie's mind was awhirl. If Mai Lay came back, she had to have been here before the abduction, Jessie thought. But when? Jessie hadn't seen her, and Ki had mentioned nothing of a previous visit. Of course Jessie had not seen Ki after he left the marshal's office for his rendezvous on the beach with Mai Lay. But then, neither had Mai Lay. Why would she have come to the hotel if she had told Ki to meet her along the beach?

There was no explanation unless . . . Jessie ran to the bed, grabbing the paper with the scorpion drawing. It was in a delicate hand, not Lord Clinton Bly's rough hand, which she remembered from when he had tried to get her to sign the power of attorney on the ship. Too, Bly had denied he was The Scorpion. She remembered him saying The Scorpion would join him in Mexico. As her thoughts raced back to every meeting with Mai Lay, Jessie remembered the night the woman called on her and Ki at the hotel. Jessie recalled Mai Lay grabbing Shaw's key to lock her door and accidentally dropping it on the floor. Had that really been an accident? When she picked up the key, had Mai Lay actually slipped the note under the door? Then came the biggest question of all.

Was Mai Lay actually The Scorpion?

Had she been left behind to kill Ki?

Jessie ran to the bed and snatched her gun, just as she heard Mai Lay's scream in the next room. Jessie raced out onto the balcony, then to the door into Ki's room. She saw Mai Lay and Ki, both naked, circling each other. In each hand, Mai Lay carried a stiletto. Even from outside, Jessie realized the stilettos were identical to the one The Scorpion had thrown at her and Wade Shaw.

Jessie barged through the door. "Hold it right there," she shouted at Mai Lay.

Mai Lay glanced at Jessie, then flung one of the narrow blades at her, but Ki slapped his hand against Mai Lay's wrist, sending her aim awry.

Jessie heard the stiletto thump into the wall behind her, and moved to get a shot at Mai Lay, but every time she would move, Mai Lay would take an opposite step, always making sure Ki was between her and Jessie.

Then, Mai Lay made a sudden lunge at Ki with the stiletto. Ki jumped backward, tripping over his clothes on the floor. He collapsed on his back, his fall saving his life as the blade would have sliced across his stomach.

In the brief instant Ki was downed, Jessie leveled her gun at Mai Lay and pulled the trigger. "That's for killing Wade

Shaw," she screamed. Though the smoke, Jessie saw a third nipple in Mai Lay's chest, this one oozing her blood and her life. Then Mai Lay tumbled forward on Ki.

He shoved her aside and scrambled up from the floor, still shaken by the close call.

"You just killed The Scorpion," he said.

"I know," she replied.

★

Chapter 21

The governor's carriage met Jessie and Ki at the train station and delivered them straight to the capitol. Galveston was far behind in miles, but not in their memories, when they pulled up in front of the stately building and were escorted by a pair of Texas Rangers into the governor's office.

The governor awaited them and greeted them somberly. "The State of Texas owes the both of you a great debt." He motioned for them to sit in the thick chairs at his worktable. "Please, tell me the whole story."

Between them, Jessie and Ki were able to relate the events that led to the destruction of Lord Clinton Bly and his evil plans.

"So there really was a Scorpion. Wade Shaw was right, God rest his soul. An armed rebellion along the Rio Grande, why, there would be severe consequences for all of us in Texas and the nation. We are forever indebted to you. How can we ever repay you, Jessie?"

"Take me to the state cemetery."

"As you wish," he replied, rising from his chair and moving with them to the door. Their footsteps echoed off the stone floor as they walked out of the capitol and into the sunshine, where the governor's carriage was waiting.

The governor joined them inside and instructed the driver where to take them. It was a short drive to the cemetery, and to the mound of newly turned dirt where Wade Shaw had been buried.

Jessie stepped from the carriage alone and walked to the grave. She stood alone with her thoughts for a moment, then returned, biting her lip. "There are politicians, governors, and heroes of the Texas Revolution buried here, but no better man than him," she said.

"He was a good man," the governor echoed.

"See that the biggest monument in this cemetery is placed over his grave. I will cover the cost."

"I will attend to that," the governor answered.

"And it is spring," Jessie continued. "See that bluebonnets are sown atop his grave, because they are as much Texas as he was."

The governor nodded, then helped Jessie back into the carriage and directed the driver to the train station. There Jessie and Ki boarded their Pullman, with the special locomotive that had been dispatched to pull it. They began the journey to the Circle Star.

It had been a long, draining trip by the time the Pullman came to a stop at the Circle Star siding. A buggy was awaiting them for the ride to the ranch house. They arrived back at the Starbuck headquarters just after noon.

Jessie stepped out of the buggy. "It's good to set foot on Circle Star land again."

Ki nodded.

"And it's still spring, when the land renews itself."

Ki nodded again.

"I think I'll saddle up and go for a long ride."

Ki could read her, knowing she wanted to be alone, so he smiled. "You've got a lot of land to cover before sundown."

She answered him with a smile, then ran to the barn.

Ki just waited. Within ten minutes she was galloping away from the ranch house toward the distant horizon, her copper-blond hair fanning out behind her in the breeze.

Ki nodded to himself. The process of renewal had begun not just for the land, but for Jessie Starbuck as well.

If you enjoyed this book, subscribe now and get...

TWO FREE

A $7.00 VALUE—

If you would like to read more of the very best, most exciting, adventurous, action-packed Westerns being published today, you'll want to subscribe to True Value's Western Home Subscription Service.

Each month the editors of True Value will select the 6 very best Westerns from America's leading publishers for special readers like you. You'll be able to preview these new titles as soon as they are published, *FREE* for ten days with no obligation!

TWO FREE BOOKS

When you subscribe, we'll send you your first month's shipment of the newest and best 6 Westerns for you to preview. With your first shipment, two of these books will be yours as our introductory gift to you absolutely *FREE* (a $7.00 value), regardless of what you decide to do. If

you like them, as much as we think you will, keep all six books but pay for just 4 at the low subscriber rate of just $2.75 each. If you decide to return them, keep 2 of the titles as our gift. No obligation.

Special Subscriber Savings

When you become a True Value subscriber you'll save money several ways. First, all regular monthly selections will be billed at the low subscriber price of just $2.75 each. That's at least a savings of $4.50 each month below the publishers price. Second, there is never any shipping, handling or other hidden charges—*Free home delivery*. What's more there is no minimum number of books you must buy, you may return any selection for full credit and you can cancel your subscription at any time. A TRUE VALUE!

A special offer for people who enjoy reading the best Westerns published today.

WESTERNS!

NO OBLIGATION

Mail the coupon below

To start your subscription and receive 2 FREE WESTERNS, fill out the coupon below and mail it today. We'll send your first shipment which includes 2 FREE BOOKS as soon as we receive it.

Mail To: **True Value Home Subscription Services, Inc. P.O. Box 5235**
120 Brighton Road, Clifton, New Jersey 07015-5235

YES! I want to start reviewing the very best Westerns being published today. Send me my first shipment of 6 Westerns for me to preview FREE for 10 days. If I decide to keep them, I'll pay for just 4 of the books at the low subscriber price of $2.75 each; a total $11.00 (a $21.00 value). Then each month I'll receive the 6 newest and best Westerns to preview Free for 10 days. If I'm not satisfied I may return them within 10 days and owe nothing. Otherwise I'll be billed at the special low subscriber rate of $2.75 each; a total of $16.50 (at least a $21.00 value) and save $4.50 off the publishers price. There are never any shipping, handling or other hidden charges. I understand I am under no obligation to purchase any number of books and I can cancel my subscription at any time, no questions asked. In any case the 2 FREE books are mine to keep.

Name

Street Address   Apt. No.

City   State   Zip Code

Telephone

Signature
(if under 18 parent or guardian must sign)

Terms and prices subject to change. Orders subject
to acceptance by True Value Home Subscription
Services, Inc.

11570-3